QUEEN CITY CANDY SHOPPE

Donna Winters

Bigwater Publishing LLC

www.GreatLakesRomances.com

Garden, Michigan

To JoAnn
who sent me North Carolina by mail
and to Roselyn
who suggested the story in the first place

Acknowledgments

I would like to thank the following for their contributions to this fictional endeavor:

First and foremost, my Lord and Savior, Jesus Christ, the source of my inspiration. He answers my prayers and makes all things possible!

And on the human level:

JoAnn Grote, who supplied historical facts and descriptions of North Carolina settings

Roselyn Smith, who proposed a two-sentence story idea for the premise of this book

Shirley and Jeannie Soest, who spent several hours sharing their knowledge of horses

Lola Sage, who took me on a long and lovely ride in her horse-drawn wagon

Shirley and Bob Slocum, who treated me to a Sunday afternoon sleigh ride on a crisp January day in 1995

Rachel Balke Heighton, who read my manuscript with unbridled enthusiasm

CONTENTS

Lake Michigan

Traverse City

Chicago

Michigan

Winston-Salem
Tanglewood

North Carolina

CHAPTER 1

Traverse City, Michigan
July 2, 1900

Coal smoke fouled the air as eighteen-year-old Rosalie Foxe slipped into a window seat aboard the half-full Grand Rapids and Indiana train bound for Detroit. She ignored the stares at her crippled right shoulder and arm as she used her left hand to set her valise on the empty seat beside her and take out the little volume of poems by John Henry Boner of her native North Carolina. Laying aside the embroidered bookmark, she started to read.

But a nightmarish accusation leveled against her earlier that morning repeated again and again in her mind. Desperate to block it out, she closed her eyes and envisioned herself in her daddy's carriage entering the long driveway at Tanglewood, the beloved North Carolina home she'd left a month ago.

The old, familiar oaks, poplars, and magnolias stretched their boughs in welcome, shading her from the blistering heat of summer in the Piedmont. Passing stables and horse pastures, she scanned the landscape for some sign of Vanda Mae, her horse-crazy sixteen-year-old sister. Was she out riding in the woods? Had her cherished mare, Tassie, produced the foal that had enticed Vanda Mae to remain in the oppressive heat rather than seek the cooler realm of the mountain resort at Blowing Rock as their mother had?

Rosalie's daydream carried her past barns and servants' quarters to the circle in front of an eighteen-room manor house that stood on a rise like a rectangular brick fortress guarding the meadow below. She hurried inside and up the sweeping staircase to the spacious bedroom that had always granted her shelter from the cruelties of the world.

The thud of a passenger car window dropping shut jolted her back to reality. She was not in North Carolina, but in northern Michigan on a sojourn that had been a graduation gift from a cherished aunt and uncle she had seldom seen in her growing-up years. Again, the contemptible words that had cast slurs on her trustworthiness and sent her packing for Tanglewood echoed in her mind. She bowed her head in a silent, urgent prayer. *Lord, right now I'm feeling like the small end of nothing whittled down to a fine point. Please carry me back to Tanglewood just as quickly as—*

"Miss Foxe, I am disappointed in you. I didn't think you'd leave Traverse City at a time like this."

Kenton McCune, the thirty-one-year-old attorney friend of her Aunt Lottie and Uncle Benjamin interrupted her supplication. He put her valise on the floor and sat on the aisle seat beside her, his neatly trimmed mustache and goatee accentuating the grim line of his mouth.

His clipped speech contrasted so sharply with the easygoing drawl of North Carolinians that it still grated on her ears despite the fact that she'd spoken with him a dozen times or more. Her gaze moved from his meticulously creased pants to his pin-tucked white shirt to his hazel-come-grey eyes.

She measured her words. "You think I stole the mortgage money from Uncle Benjamin and Aunt Lottie, don't you now?"

Kenton leaned close. *"Did* you?"

The question and his nearness augmented her discomfort. "You'd have to be crazy as a betsy bug to think I'd do that. I made the payment on the candy store Friday morning, just like they asked me to."

"You're sure?"

Rosalie glared at him, then raised her book between them in an effort to ignore his question, the scent of his sandalwood soap that reminded her so much of her daddy, and the peculiar effect this Michigander was having on her nerves.

Kenton lowered the book with one finger—the nailless one he'd smashed in a baseball game awhile back. But he'd hit a home run in that game and she could still see him dashing around the bases.

He continued. "Running away makes you look guilty. Tell me again you didn't take the money."

Rosalie sighed heavily. "I did *not* take it, Mr. McCune. Now, are you satisfied?"

"No. Not until you get off this train. You're the only person who can help me keep Gowen from foreclosing on Ben and Lottie." He paused, his expression more solemn. "Besides, your aunt and uncle will be deeply hurt to think you've abandoned them."

Rosalie snapped her book shut forgetting to replace the bookmark still on her lap. "You may be a smooth-talking Yankee lawyer from Harvard, Mr. McCune, but that butters no cornbread with me at-all. I mean, do you really think you can convince me to stay?"

Kenton picked up the bookmark and read it aloud. "'Do unto others as you would have others do unto you.' Did you make this?" He waved it in front of her. "Or did you steal it?"

Rosalie snatched it from him. "Of course I made it! I try to live by its motto, too."

"Then live by it now. See this thing through. You can't run from your troubles, Miss Foxe."

She looked away.

He drew a deep breath. "The city is about to fill up with guests for the Independence Day celebration. Ben and Lottie need your help at the store more than ever. Besides, you promised to attend the Carnival Ball with me tomorrow night."

Placing the bookmark inside the front cover, Rosalie focused on him. "My mind is made up. I'm going home to Vanda Mae and Daddy. I miss them something fierce. I miss Shani's grits and red-eye gravy. *Most* of all, I miss Willy Jo Winthrop." She named her neighbor and best friend, the twenty-two-year-old next door.

"But—"

"I know you only invited me to the ball to please Aunt Lottie. I never wanted to go in the first place. The sooner I get away from here, the better." The instant the words came out, she regretted speaking falsely—about her desire to go to the ball at least. Only a distinguished few had been invited and she had counted it a privilege not to be relegated to the gallery like the rest of the public.

Kenton glared at her.

She fidgeted with the satin bow at her neck, the one with the crimped tails she always wore. For an instant she was sure he'd grab hold of that ribbon and lead her off the train.

"Go home to Tanglewood, then. I'll give Ben and Lottie your good byes." He made his way toward the exit at the back of the car.

Rosalie turned to watch him go, her stomach churning. He was right. She couldn't outrun trouble.

He disappeared from view just as the conductor shouted, "Last call! All aboard!"

~~~

As the train rumbled out of the station, Kenton paused beside his carriage and talked to his grey gelding like he always did when trying to sort out his options.

"She's gone, Judge. What do you make of that?"

The animal snorted and bobbed his head.

"All right, so you're glad. I know she hurt your feelings, the way she carried on about your color when she first came to town." He took hold of the horse's bridle and patted his nose. "Trouble is, I don't know what I'm going to tell Ben and Lottie."

He was about to climb into his carriage when he spotted Rosalie a few feet away looking as forlorn as faded forget-me-nots. He wanted to scold her for the worry she'd caused but thought better of it.

Hesitantly, she approached him. "You can tell Aunt Lottie and Uncle Benjamin that your only witness has postponed her return to North Carolina and is walking home from the station."

She seemed so vulnerable standing beside his rig, her valise hanging from her left hand, her right arm clutched tight against her side. He took her bag. "I'll drive you home. You can tell them yourself."

Her brown eyes flashed. "You know very well I'll never ride behind that grey gelding of yours—or anyone else's!"

He sighed. "I thought maybe this time would be different."

"I changed my mind about leaving, but I haven't changed my mind about grey horses."

He set her bag in the carriage. "I'd think you could trust Judge by now. You've known him long enough."

"A lifetime wouldn't be enough. I'm still paying for the last time I trusted a grey horse—a gelding like Judge—six years ago." She rubbed her right shoulder as if remembering the day she'd fallen and become permanently injured.

"You can't tell a horse by its color, Miss Foxe." He paused, struggling to suppress his frustration. "I'm sorry you fell off your gelding, but there's no logic in avoiding grey horses for the rest of your life."

She laughed. "I know that, Mr. McCune. I never claimed to be logical. I allow my emotions to be my guide, and right now they're telling me to take a nice, leisurely walk beside this fresh water bay you Michigan Yanks are so fond of while I think about the fine mess I'm in." She turned and strode away.

Kenton climbed aboard his rig. As he drove toward Ben and Lottie Marshall's Queen City Candy Shoppe, he took mental account of his day. Despite continuing sunshine, it now seemed clouded with trouble over a certain North Carolina miss, and the problems of his dear friends. Foul weather had moved in with the phone call he'd received from the middle-aged bachelor brother and spinster sister less than an hour earlier telling him about Cutler Gowen's visit, his threat to foreclose at the end of the month, and the discovery that as a result, Rosalie had departed for home with one small bag, leaving a note to forward her trunks. Ben, with no rig of his own and the knowledge that Rosalie planned to leave on the eleven fifteen train, had placed the urgent call and asked Kenton to intervene.

Aside from preventing the young miss's escape, Kenton was deeply troubled over Gowen's eagerness to evict the Marshalls from their property. The entrepreneur had arrived in town months ago, taken over the mortgage on the Marshalls' Front Street shop from its previous owner—as a favor to the Newtons who needed cash, so he said—then proceeded to purchase a parcel a few blocks west of it and erect his American Candy Company factory. Although the Marshalls made the bulk of their profits on fudge, avoiding direct competition with the hard candies that Gowen produced and sold wholesale, his threat to close them down now seemed to suggest ulterior motives from the very start.

Kenton parked in front of the Marshalls' confectionery, picked up Rosalie's valise, and headed inside. The warm day seemed even hotter in the store where Lottie, whose round form stretched the limits of her white dress and apron, stood behind the glass case weighing roasted nuts for a customer. Ben was cooling a batch of vanilla fudge—Kenton's favorite—on the marble table in the center of the store, perspiration trickling down his plump cheeks to dampen his white, collarless shirt. Both paused in their duties the moment they saw him.

Lottie was the first to speak, fussing with the neck strap of her apron as she focused a worried look on the bag he carried. "Is that valise all you found of Rosalie?"

Ben spoke before Kenton could answer. "She's gone back to Tanglewood. I knew it." He tossed down his spatula, embedding it in the mound of fudge.

Kenton shook his head. "She's still in Traverse City. I tried to drive her home, but you know how she is about Judge."

Finished with her customer, Lottie turned to Kenton. "Right skittish. I'd forgotten about that when Ben rang you up."

Ben peeled off his wire glasses and mopped the sweat from his forehead and nose. "I suppose she insisted on walking home."

Kenton nodded. "I'll set her bag in the back."

Ben put on his glasses and stuffed his handkerchief into the pocket of his baggy white pants. "While you're here, you might want to take a look at that notice from Mr. Gowen. It's on the back table."

Kenton had set the bag beneath the table in the back room and was reading through the eviction notice when Ben joined him.

Closing the door to the shop, the confectioner spoke in confident tones. "I'm sure Rosalie made the payment like I asked her to."

"You're absolutely certain?"

"I had a long talk with her after Cutler Gowen came by." He tapped the eviction notice. "She remembered some things about her trip to his office that I think you'll find very intriguing." With a sudden change of topic, Ben asked, "Did I tell you Erik and Bridget Olson were here from Omena last week to pick up a load of fudge for The Clovers?"

Kenton shook his head, unwilling to discuss mutual friends just now. "Ben, about your niece."

He scowled. "Patience, Kenton. This is all part of the same recipe." A smile began to emerge. "The Olsons inquired about you and said to give you their regards. If they aren't the happiest-looking newlywed pair I ever did see . . ." The smile faded and once again, Ben seemed all business. "The payment they gave me for the fudge will be of particular interest to you."

When Ben had finished sharing his information about the Olson money and other details Rosalie had described about her trip to Cutler Gowen's office, Kenton asked to see the mortgage agreement. Within minutes he had verified the requirement for only thirty days' notice of eviction upon failure to make a payment, and the complete lack of a grace period within which to bring the loan up to date.

Deciding on a course of action, Kenton told Ben, "I can see this won't wait until your niece is done with her walk. I'm going to find her."

"With that grey gelding of yours?"

Kenton shrugged, heading out the door with the knowledge that Miss Foxe's fear of his horse was a minor inconvenience compared with the trouble over the Marshalls' mortgage.

Driving immediately to the Germaine Brothers livery, Kenton parked his own rig and rented a buggy hitched to a chestnut mare, then spent his lunch hour in search of Rosalie. He found her not near the bay, but in Hannah Park on Sixth Street across from Mr. Hannah's Queen Ann mansion. She was sitting on a bench feeding the ducks near the Boardman River.

Kenton sat down beside her. "I've just had a talk with your uncle. I understand you paid his mortgage with a twenty-dollar gold piece."

She continued tossing scraps of stale bread to the ducks, speaking to them by name. Her attention still on the hungry fowl, she said, "That double eagle had a nick in it."

"On the edge near the word 'God.' Your uncle mentioned that."

She tossed out the last of her bread and turned to Kenton. "'In God We Trust.' Seems ironic, putting it on gold and silver coins. I mean, if we really trust in God, why do we rely so much on money?"

"Would you recognize it again if you saw it?"

"Do you believe in God, Mr. McCune?"

"That's not the question right now. The question—"

"Of course I'd recognize it if I saw it. I've hardly thought of anything else since Mr. Gowen marched into the candy shop this morning."

"Then we must go to Mr. Gowen's factory right now and straighten this thing out." Kenton started to get up, but Rosalie's next words stopped him.

"It won't do us a lick of good. That Hackbardt woman who works as Mr. Gowen's secretary stole that coin and has no intention of letting anyone catch her."

Kenton considered the accusation, and the fact that he'd recommended Clarissa Hackbardt as secretary to Cutler Gowen last month, despite the problems she'd caused for the Olsons before their marriage. The young Wisconsin woman had convinced him that her days as a schemer and conniver were all in the past, and that she would make an excellent assistant to the entrepreneur. Kenton couldn't assume Clarissa's guilt with no evidence, especially since, to his knowledge, she had no past history of mishandling money.

"Do *you* believe in God, Miss Foxe?"

The firm set to Rosalie's chin softened. "Of course I believe in God, but I doubt very much that will have any effect at all on circumstances involving the likes of Miss Hackbardt."

"'Judge not, lest ye be judged,' Miss Foxe. Let's pay a call on Miss Hackbardt and allow her to answer for herself."

CHAPTER 2

On the ride to Cutler Gowen's factory, Rosalie answered Kenton's questions about her previous visit there to make the mortgage payment, reiterating the details she had shared with her Uncle Benjamin earlier, such as the fact that Cutler Gowen's secretary had marked the payment down in a ledger book, and that she had offered no receipt. When they arrived at their destination, she preceded Kenton through the door.

The Hackbardt woman was sitting behind her large oak desk at the rear of the small reception area, her hair coiffed perfectly in a Gibson Girl pouf, her white blouse spotless and without a wrinkle. She looked just as she had when Rosalie had brought the mortgage payment, and like before, the heavy scent of rose perfume hung in the air.

Clarissa greeted them cordially. "Mr. McCune, Miss . . ."

Rosalie reintroduced herself. "I'm Miss Foxe, the niece of Benjamin and Lottie Marshall. I came here Friday morning to make the mortgage payment on their store." Recollections of the woman staring openly at her crippled arm as she was now doing, came flooding back.

Clarissa rose, offering a smile Rosalie found insincere. "Forgive me. I have a *terrible* memory."

Rosalie ignored the smile. "I suppose then, you haven't any memory at-all of my coming here."

In imitation of Rosalie's southern drawl, Clarissa said, "None at-all, Miss . . . Foxe, was it?"

Rosalie was about to accuse the woman of outright deceit when Kenton spoke up. "Miss Hackbardt, Miss Foxe assures me that you marked the payment down in a ledger. If you'll check your book, I'm confident we can resolve this problem."

"Certainly, Mr. McCune. I should have thought of that." Clarissa stepped up to a bookcase lined with leather-bound volumes and extracted a burgundy one with the year '1900' imprinted in gold on the spine. Opening to the page with the most recent entries, she searched the listings, then turned the book around and set it in front of Kenton. "I'm sorry. I find no record of payment on the Marshalls' mortgage for the current month."

"Why am I not at-all surprised?" Rosalie's sarcasm cut the air.

Clarissa flashed a wicked smile which turned suddenly sweet when Kenton had finished his study of the page and addressed her again. "I'd like to speak with Mr. Gowen."

"He's with a—"

Kenton cut her off. "We'll wait."

Clarissa closed the ledger. "But you have no appointment."

Kenton leaned forward. "My business will take but a minute. We're not leaving until I speak with him."

She indicated the empty chairs. "Suit yourselves." She sat down to her typewriter, filling the office with the slow rhythm of its tap . . . tap . . . tap.

Rosalie fidgeted with her lace gloves, occasionally exchanging glances with Kenton, who was checking the gold cufflinks in his French cuffs at least once every minute. She privately concluded that her own single-handed proficiency on the typewriter could surpass Clarissa's two-finger method by several words per minute.

Suddenly, the door to Cutler Gowen's office opened and the entrepreneur—his dark, wavy hair plastered against his head with a heavily scented pomade— emerged with his client.

While Clarissa saw the broad-shouldered, auburn-haired visitor out, Kenton rose to face Gowen.

The other man spoke first. "McCune, I was certain you'd show up here before this day was out, and you haven't disappointed me."

"About the Marshalls' eviction notice—"

Rosalie stepped face to face with Gowen. "You had no right, Mr. Gowen. No right at-all to tell my Uncle Benjamin and Aunt Lottie to leave their store when they've made every payment on time."

"Now, now, Miss Foxe." Gowen spoke in soothing, golden tones. "I can certainly understand your distress, since the money for the payment was evidently entrusted to you."

"And I entrusted it to your secretary! It was a double eagle with—"

Kenton cut her off. "Miss Foxe, enough said."

Gowen clucked his tongue. "Lies always catch up with their perpetrator, Miss Foxe."

Rosalie drew a sharp breath to respond, but Kenton intervened. "Mr. Gowen, you maintain that the Marshalls' mortgage is in arrears." He pulled the eviction notice from his pocket and laid a shiny new double eagle on top of it. "Let me make the payment now. What difference can one day make?"

"All the difference, McCune."

Rosalie strode to Clarissa's desk and began opening drawers. Frustrated with the limited use of her right hand, she made her left hand work faster, searching the contents, tossing papers, pen nibs, seals, and rubber stamps in a heap on the blotter.

Gowen didn't flinch. "Theatrics won't convince anyone of your innocence, Miss Foxe. I suspect you kept the twenty dollars for a hat or some other fancy goods at Hamilton and Milliken."

Rosalie was about to argue when Clarissa came through the door. "Miss Foxe! Just what do you think you're doing?" She stormed across the room.

Gowen caught her by the arm. "Let her be, Miss Hackbardt. You and I both know she's looking for something that's not there."

Having searched the last drawer, Rosalie slammed it shut, and turned to Gowen. "I reckon that coin's a lost ball in high weeds now, but I had to look, anyway."

Kenton took Rosalie by the elbow. "We're finished here, Miss Foxe. Let's be on our way."

Gowen preceded them to the door, holding it open graciously. "Excellent idea, McCune. And Miss Foxe, you might as well tell your aunt and uncle to start packing. At the end of the month they'll be moving elsewhere."

Rosalie paused on the threshold to give him a sharp look. "You know what I think, Mr. Gowen? I think you're slicker than a bucket of boiled okra, but you'd better watch out. One day, you'll be sipping sorrow with a teaspoon."

As the door closed behind them, Clarissa's sing-songy voice mimicked her final words in an exaggerated drawl. A knot formed in Rosalie's throat. The thought of her aunt and uncle being put out of their home and business by the likes of Clarissa Hackbardt and Cutler Gowen provoked her to tears.

Outside the door, Kenton paused, taking her by the shoulders. Immediately, she shrugged off his hands and looked down, unable to bear anyone but Willy Jo Winthrop touching her imperfect arm.

Kenton lifted her chin, forcing her to meet his gaze. "Don't put me off, Miss Foxe. I meant no offense."

Her throat constricted tighter still, making it impossible to speak.

He continued. "I'm not about to let Gowen get away with this. If it wouldn't inconvenience you, I'd like to make an inquiry at the bank now. Maybe the double eagle with the nick in it will turn up, and someone might remember Miss Hackbardt or Mr. Gowen making the deposit."

Rosalie nodded, her glum mood brightening as she rode the two blocks to the bank. She had accompanied her aunt and uncle here many times during the past month to make deposits from the candy shop. Her father's draft from People's National Bank in Winston-Salem had been deposited here, too, for her to draw on to cover her expenses during her northern sojourn. She was thankful that Mr. Johnson, the president of the First National Bank, was a cheerful sort. He greeted her by name as she crossed the marble floor to his desk, then he spoke to Kenton.

"How can I be of service on this bright, sunshiny day?" He waited until his guests had been seated, then sat again in the chair behind his desk.

Kenton explained. "Our request is a rather odd one, but important . . ."

Mr. Johnson fussed with his bow tie as he listened, then he asked a clerk to gather together all the double eagles on the premises. But when Rosalie and Kenton inspected them, none had a nick near the word "God."

Mr. Johnson accompanied them to the door. "I'm sorry to think the Marshalls might lose their shop. The hard candy from that new factory in town has its appeal, but it certainly can't compare to the fudge and other sweets the Marshalls put out." He paused at the door. "I know that for a fact, and not because I bought any of Gowen's goods. He was in here the other day handing out horehounds and lemon drops."

Rosalie spoke up. "I'll tell you what I think, Mr. Johnson. I think Mr. Gowen is eager to take over Uncle Benjamin and Aunt Lottie's shop so he can put his own goods in there."

Kenton pressed his hand against Rosalie's back. "Miss Foxe, we'd best be on our way."

Rosalie stalled. "Mr. McCune, do you mean to imply you think I'm wrong?"

Kenton smiled. "Quite the opposite. I think you're right, and I think we'd best keep looking for that coin." To Mr. Johnson, he said, "You'll keep your eye out for it, won't you?"

Mr. Johnson nodded. "I'll be in touch the moment it comes through."

On the way to the rig, Kenton told Rosalie, "I can think of a couple of places where that coin might be. One of them is relatively easy to investigate. The other is next to impossible."

Rosalie stepped into the carriage. "I'd give a small fortune to take a look through Miss Hackbardt's personal possessions right now."

Kenton settled beside her and set the buggy on a southward path along Cass Street. "I can't promise you'll get the chance to go through Clarissa's things for yourself, but I know a couple of ladies who can be persuaded to investigate for us, and they won't charge one penny." He continued straight until making a left turn onto Washington Street.

"Mr. McCune, if you don't mind my asking, exactly where are you taking me?"

"Are you any good at euchre, Miss Foxe?"

"My Aunt Ophelia says a deck of cards is the devil's prayer book," Rosalie informed him, adding with a laugh, "but I'm better at euchre than I am at hearts."

He chuckled. "Then I suggest you keep that a secret from the Doyle sisters."

"Are you saying a few hands of euchre will give us the access we desire?"

"You're a very bright young woman, Miss Foxe."

"Bright enough to know when to lose."

"You took the words right out of my mouth."

Kenton pulled up in front of a sign that read, "Doyle Sisters Rooming House." The modest home had been freshly painted sea green with fuchsia and violet trim. Despite the colorful exterior, Rosalie found the interior pale, with ivory lace at the windows and a dusty rose pattern on the parlor sofa and chairs. True to Kenton's prediction, the cards were brought out and a game of euchre was required before Miss Ava and Miss Eda would permit discussion of the real reason for his visit. The steeple clock on the mantel had struck a quarter past four by the time he had explained about the missing double eagle and the consequences to the Marshalls.

Kenton spoke cautiously. "So you can see why we're wondering if there's any possibility you would consider looking in Clarissa's room for the coin."

Miss Ava blinked rapidly. "I would never consider going through Miss Hackbardt's personal belongings. Would you, Eda?"

Miss Eda touched her lace handkerchief to each of her temples. "Of course not, sister."

Miss Ava blinked some more. "You do understand, don't you, Mr. McCune? Why, if word got out that we were so nosy as to go through our boarders' things, not a soul would come to stay with—."

Miss Eda interrupted. "But sister, have you forgotten? We were planning to give Miss Hackbardt's room a thorough cleaning this very afternoon."

Miss Ava thought a moment. "Eda, your memory is a constant source of amazement to me. We'd best fetch the carpet sweeper and dust rags this very minute, and I think we should ask Mr. McCune and Miss Foxe to come upstairs and supervise, lest we miss any dirt or cobwebs."

Rosalie and Kenton followed the sisters up the stairs to a bedroom at the rear of the house. A jewelry box on the dresser immediately aroused Rosalie's curiosity, piqued further when Miss Ava dusted its cover, but showed no inclination to look inside.

Meanwhile, Eda had started on the secretary. After dusting its shelves of books and bric-a-brac, she tried to open the slant top but found it locked. Touching her finger to the empty keyhole, she said, "Sister, I don't suppose we have an extra key to this desk, have we? I'd be remiss in my duties if I didn't straighten up inside for Miss Hackbardt."

Miss Ava sighed. "I fear not."

Unable to restrain herself, Rosalie took a hat pin from a cushion on the dresser. "I'll take a stab at that lock, Miss Eda." Using her left hand, she unlocked the desk within seconds.

Kenton eyed her curiously. "How did you do that so quickly?"

Miss Eda's eyes grew wide. "Yes, how *did* you do that? You're awfully clever for one with . . . who . . .."

Rosalie grinned. "I've picked much tougher locks than that single-handed, so to speak. I learned it from Gaspar, Daddy's hired man. He was an escape artist with a circus side show before Daddy hired him to take care of his horses."

Kenton chuckled. "I never would have guessed that answer."

Eda said, "Nor would I." Turning her attention to the desk, she began tidying it up, searching every pigeonhole thoroughly. She had removed a crystal paperweight and appeared to be on the brink of a question when Miss Ava held up a pair of white lace gloves she had found in a dresser drawer.

"Eda, look. Aren't these the brand new gloves you were missing last week?" She handed them to her sister.

Eda offered the paperweight in exchange. "And we were looking high and low for this a few days ago. We turned the place upside down in search of it—all except for this room. Remember?"

Ava's eyes sparkled as she cradled the piece of etched crystal in her hands. "Mother's Steuben paperweight. I'd given up hope of ever seeing it again."

Eda said, "You even asked Miss Hackbardt if she'd seen it, and she denied any knowledge of its whereabouts."

Following a moment's thought, Ava said, "Eda, you and I are going to have to do a much more thorough cleaning than we had planned."

"Sister, do you mean what I think you mean?"

Ava nodded. To Rosalie, she said, "Would you be so good as to take mother's paperweight downstairs and set it on the center table in the parlor? And Mr. McCune, would you please fetch Miss Hackbardt's trunk from the attic? We must start packing her things immediately. She'll soon be home from Mr. Gowen's office."

When Kenton had fetched the trunk, Rosalie helped the Doyles fill it with Clarissa's belongings. They emptied the desk and dresser drawers, and had packed up all but the jewelry case when Eda went to set it in the trunk.

Ava stopped her sister. "I think we'd best look inside this." Setting it on the dresser again, she tried the clasp, but it was locked. She offered Rosalie a hat pin. "Do you mind?"

In less time than Rosalie had needed to open the desk, she had released the clasp and begun to lift the lid. A music box started up, sending the tinkling strains of *After the Ball is Over* into the room. With Kenton, Eda, and Ava looking on, Rosalie opened the top wide.

She had been so certain she'd find the double eagle, but there was no sign of money in the velvet lined tray, only some cheap paste lapel pins and a mother-of-pearl cameo.

Ava blinked rapidly. "I don't see anything of ours in there, do you, Eda?"

She touched her handkerchief to each temple. "No, sister."

The music box wound down as Rosalie started to close the lid. Kenton stopped her, his hand covering hers.

"It looks like there's another compartment beneath the tray."

Warmth flowed through Rosalie. Was it Kenton's touch, or her anticipation of what they might find?

As he began lifting the tray from the box, Clarissa's voice floated up the staircase. "Miss Ava? Miss Eda? Anybody home?

CHAPTER 3

Rosalie stared at the three gold coins in the bottom of Clarissa Hackbardt's jewelry box. Her heart plummeted to the floor. None of them was a double eagle.

Kenton shut the box while Ava and Eda answered Clarissa's call from the front hallway in turn.

"Come upstairs, Miss Hackbardt!"

"We have a surprise for you!"

Ava set the jewelry case in the trunk and closed the lid. "Mr. McCune, would you be so kind as to fasten the straps, please?"

Kenton immediately obliged. He was still tightening the last buckle when Clarissa reached the door to her room, her face a puzzle. "Mr. McCune, what are you doing with my trunk?"

Before he could answer, Ava said, "Miss Hackbardt, I trust you have friends you can stay with tonight."

Eda spoke next. "If not, the Park Place has nice rooms, so I've been told."

Rosalie couldn't help smiling. "It's just as well you're moving out, Miss Hackbardt. I'll be in need of a place, should Mr. Gowen put me and my kin out on the street. Your room should suit just fine, if need be."

Clarissa put her hands on her hips. "So that's what this is all about. A twenty-dollar gold piece that doesn't even exist."

Ava's eyelashes fluttered. "This is about my mother's paperweight."

Eda dabbed her temple with her handkerchief. "And my brand new lace gloves."

Clarissa sighed. "I only borrowed them. If you wanted them back, all you had to do was ask."

Ava said, "I *did* ask. Just last week. You told me you hadn't seen the paperweight."

Clarissa seemed about to argue when Eda spoke again. "We can't countenance behavior such as yours from our guests. You owe us fifty cents for room and board this week, due now." She put out her hand.

Clarissa reached in her pocket and handed Miss Eda a half-dollar.

Kenton hoisted her trunk to his shoulder. "I'll carry this downstairs for you, Miss Hackbardt. You'd best ring up Germaine Brothers to have it transferred."

The dinner hour was fast approaching, and when Clarissa finished using the telephone, Rosalie rang up Ben and Lottie to let them know she'd be late for the evening meal. Seven o'clock had come and gone by the time Clarissa and her trunk departed.

The Doyle sisters saw Kenton and Rosalie to the door, Miss Ava blinking furiously as she spoke. "Miss Foxe, you're welcome to take up quarters in Miss Hackbardt's old room. We'd enjoy your company."

Eda said, "We could get up a game of cutthroat euchre every afternoon."

Rosalie smiled. "Thank you, ladies, for the offer, but
I'm of a mind to prove to Mr. Gowen that I made that
mortgage payment before he can put me and my aunt
and uncle out on the street."

As Kenton drove Rosalie home, she began to recall
their earlier conversation. "On the way to the Doyles',
you said there were two likely places the coin might be
found. We've eliminated one possibility. What's the other one?"

"Where would *you* look next?"

Rosalie thought a moment. "I'd look through Cutler
Gowen's office."

Kenton smiled. "The more time you spend with me,
the more your mind works like mine. Just look at how
far you've come since this morning!"

Rosalie chuckled. "All the way from the train depot.
That's at least two blocks from here, isn't it?"

Kenton laughed. "At least."

When the lighthearted moment had passed, Rosalie
said, "About Mr. Gowen's office. I don't suppose there's
any way at-all I could get in there for a look-see, is
there?"

Kenton scratched his goatee.

"Can you get the police to search it?"

Still thoughtful, Kenton stated, "We have only your
word that you made the payment. No proof, not even a
receipt."

Rosalie sighed. "I sure got my tail in a crack this time.
I wish I were back home. My uncle's the sheriff of For-

syth County. He'd get things straightened out real quick."

Brows furrowed, Kenton asked, "You aren't thinking of running off again, are you?"

Rosalie shook her head, still mulling over her quandary as Kenton pulled the rig to a halt in front of Marshalls' shop. He started to get out, but Rosalie stopped him, her hand on his arm. "Mr. McCune, I just thought of something. I wonder if the cleaning lady at Mr. Gowen's office has seen anything at-all that could help us?"

Taking her hand in his, Kenton said, "There's little chance of that, but I suppose it wouldn't hurt to ask. Mrs. Potter—Constance Potter—cleans the office there and at several other buildings around town, mine included. Now let me see you to the door." He started to let go of her hand, but without aforethought, she held tight.

"I'm going to ring up Mrs. Potter tonight and inquire. Time's a-wasting, Mr. McCune. I've got to try *something!*"

He looked down at the hand clutching his.

Rosalie's face grew warm and she tried to let go, but it was he who prolonged the contact this time, firmly squeezing her fingers.

He spoke in a calm, but compelling tone. "Promise me you won't run home to North Carolina just yet, and that you'll stay clear of Gowen's office."

Rosalie nodded, instantly regretful that she had agreed to the second half of the promise.

"And one more thing. You *are* still going to the ball with me, aren't you?"

She smiled. "I have no reason at-all not to."

"Good. Now let me help you down."

When he walked her to the door, Aunt Lottie called to him from the upstairs window. "Thanks for bringing Rosalie home, Mr. McCune. Will you stay to supper? I've kept the hash and eggs hot, and there's plenty for the two of you."

Kenton gazed up at Aunt Lottie. "I can't stay tonight. Thanks, anyway." To Rosalie, he said, "I'll see you soon. Now you'd better go upstairs and tell your aunt and uncle what's happened today."

~~~

Rosalie had little appetite for the hash and eggs her aunt served up, but she managed a forkful at a time amidst a description of her visit to Gowen's office and her encounter with the Hackbardt woman. Recalling Gowen's parting words, she set down her fork and focused on her uncle.

"Mr. Gowen had a message for you. He said you might as well start packing. At the end of the month you'll be moving elsewhere."

The furrow in her uncle's brow lingered only a moment. "That's presumptuous. And preposterous."

Lottie nodded. "Mr. McCune will prevail on our behalf. In fact, I'm confident he'll settle the whole matter before week's end."

Rosalie sighed. "But to do that, he'll have to locate the coin I gave Miss Hackbardt. Considering what we've been through today, that's about as likely as a sow standing up on her hind legs and doing a ballet." She described their investigations concerning Clarissa.

When she had finished her explanation and her supper, her uncle said, "That coin can't have gone far. I have faith that regardless of the way things seem right now, Mr. McCune will find it soon and everything will work out."

Lottie said, "I can't believe the Lord would allow us to be put out on the street. Not when we've been perfectly regular in our payments and honest in all our dealings."

Rosalie bit back the argument on her tongue. "I pray you're right."

Determined to keep looking for the coin despite her aunt's and her uncle's complacency, she began to formulate a plan for action as she helped them with the supper dishes. When the last of the pots and pans had been put away, Ben retired to the sitting room to take up his reading. With her aunt still fussing in the kitchen, she looked up the telephone number for Mrs. Constance Potter, then picked up the phone and asked the operator to make the connection.

While she waited for the cleaning woman to come on the line, Lottie asked in a half-whisper, "Who are you ringing up?"

Rosalie whispered, "I'll tell you in a minute."

Then the scratchy voice of an elderly woman grated over the wire. "Hello?"

"Mrs. Potter?"

"Who's this?"

"Rosalie Foxe. I'm an acquaintance of Mr. McCune. He said maybe you could help me."

"Rosalie who? Foxe? You sound like one of those Dixie belles that comes up here to get out of the heat."

Rosalie spoke as quickly as she could in an attempt to overcome her southern drawl. "I'm from North Carolina and I'm visiting my aunt and uncle, Benjamin and Lottie Marshall. They own the—"

"I know, I know. The confectionery. What are you ringing me up for, anyway? I can't take on any more cleaning jobs just now."

"That's not why I rang you up. Mr. McCune said you might be able to help me. I understand you do the cleaning in Mr. Gowen's office at the American Candy Company."

"That's right."

"Well, I'm looking for a coin that was misplaced there—"

"Well I didn't steal it! You've got your nerve, ringing me up and accusing me of such a thing!" She slammed down the phone.

Rosalie immediately asked the operator to ring Mrs. Potter again. The moment she answered, Rosalie said, "I know you didn't steal anything, Mrs. Potter! Now please don't hang up! My aunt and uncle will lose their store if I don't find that coin!"

Mrs. Potter drew a deep breath. "You'd better explain yourself, girl, and quick, because right now you sound like you're in need of a vacation at the asylum."

Rosalie told her about the payment made with a coin marred by a nick and Gowen's claim of nonpayment and his threat to foreclose on the Queen City Candy Shoppe. The look of disapproval on her aunt's face couldn't diminish the effect of Mrs. Potter's reaction.

"Why, that rascal, Gowen! You don't mean to let him get away with this, do you?"

"No, ma'am! But I can't do anything at-all now, unless I have your help." Rosalie told of her unsuccessful search for the coin at the bank, and in the Hackbardt woman's desk, jewelry case, and room.

Rosalie continued. "Mrs. Potter, I'm wondering if you'll let me help you when you clean Mr. Gowen's office next time. With two of us looking, maybe we'll find what I'm after."

A pause followed, then the woman replied, "I work alone. Can't have you getting underfoot. Besides, I start at five tomorrow morning—too early for anyone but the birds. I'll let you know if I find that coin, though."

"I can be there at five!" Rosalie insisted. "I help my aunt and uncle make their candy at that hour every morning. I'll work with you tomorrow instead. I don't expect to be paid."

Patiently, Rosalie listened to Mrs. Potter's labored breathing in one ear and her aunt's whispered protests in the other. She covered the mouthpiece so the cleaning woman wouldn't hear Lottie, and waited for a reply.

With resignation, Mrs. Potter finally said, "I guess it's all right. I've got to warn you, though, Gowen keeps everything locked—his desk, file cabinets, and closet. This will likely be a waste of your time."

"I'll take that chance." Rosalie said hastily.

"Then meet me at the back door of the factory at five sharp." She hung up.

Rosalie hadn't even finished placing the receiver on its hook when Lottie began her protest. "You can't go to work with Mrs. Potter. What would your folks say, you taking up work as a common cleaning woman?" Without waiting for a reply, she called her brother. "Ben, come in here and talk some sense into this niece of ours!" She fingered the neck strap of her apron while she waited, starting in again as soon as he reached the door. "Rosalie intends to hire herself out—"

"I heard," he said impatiently, placing a marker in the book he'd been reading.

"Tell her she can't go!"

"For the love of fudge, Lottie, I don't know why you're so upset. Rosalie's a full-grown young woman now. If she wants to go clean Gowen's office at five in the morning, I don't see why we should stop her."

Rosalie smiled. "Thank you, Uncle Benjamin. I knew you'd understand."

Lottie scowled at her brother. "We can't let her go out alone at that hour. It's not even light out!"

"I'll walk her down to the factory. Now, if you don't mind, I'm going back to my story."

Lottie focused on Rosalie. "Does Kenton know you plan to do this?"

Rosalie winced. She'd promised to stay clear of Gowen's office, but a larger issue was at stake. "He's the one who told me about Mrs. Potter in the first place. Now don't you fret. Nothing at-all will go wrong."

Lottie continued to fuss with her apron strap. "There must be a better way."

"I can't think of one. Good night, Aunt Lottie."

Rosalie retired to her small sleeping chamber off the storage room at the rear of the first floor, her thoughts fixed on events to come as she drifted off to sleep. When she arose and dressed in the early morning hours, she slipped the set of lock picks Gaspar had given her years ago into her apron pocket, and gathered a bucketful of cleaning supplies from the back room. At breakfast, served at half-past four when her aunt and uncle rose to get an early start on their candy-making for the day, barely a word was exchanged.

The sun had just peeked over the horizon, sending muted orange streaks low across the bay, when she set out with her uncle for the American Candy Company. Kerchief covering her hair, she walked briskly along Front Street. A warm, gentle breeze caused her apron to flutter, and despite pressing thoughts of her mission, she couldn't miss the enticing aroma of fresh bread when she passed the bakery, or the quiet tinkling of bottles as the milk man made his rounds.

Pausing at the rear door of the factory, Ben set down the bucket he'd carried for her and waited with her for Mrs. Potter. Moments later, a wide-hipped woman waddled toward them through the alley, her shoulders dipping alternately with each step.

Ben put the bucket in Rosalie's hand. "There's Mrs. Potter. I'll see you later." He set off for the confectionery leaving Rosalie to introduce herself.

"Good morning, Mrs. Potter. I'm Rosalie Foxe."

"Hmph," came the reply. Using one of the keys tied to the end of her apron string, she opened the back door and led the way through a series of halls. In the light of Gowen's office, she stared for a moment at Rosalie's crippled right arm, but her words concerned only the cleaning chores.

Quickly, she directed a thorough cleaning of books and book shelves, rugs and mats, pictures and light fixtures. Rosalie was dying to peek inside Gowen's locked desk, file cabinets, and closet. She fingered the set of lock picks in her apron pocket and toyed with the idea of opening a desk drawer while Mrs. Potter waxed the floor in the reception area, but decided against it.

Two hours had passed when the woman gathered rags and feather duster, lemon oil and paste wax into her bucket. "Sorry we didn't find your coin, Miss Foxe. But I warned you last night, Mr. Gowen keeps things locked pretty tight. Now, I've got to get on to the bank and do some cleaning there."

Outside the back door, Rosalie spoke while Mrs. Potter locked up. "Thank you for allowing me to help. Sorry we got nothing more than what the bear grabbed at."

The woman's mouth quirked into a smile. "Don't take no offense, but you get more accomplished with that one good hand of yours than most womenfolk who've got two. You can work with me anytime you want."

Rosalie smiled. "Thank you, Mrs. Potter. I consider that a real compliment." She stepped off with the woman, accompanying her until she disappeared inside the bank.

Doing an about face, Rosalie returned to the back door of the candy factory. She checked to see that no one else was in the alley, then took out the lock picks and swiftly regained access to the building. The door to Gowen's office opened with equal ease. Immediately, she went to the closet. One pick at a time, she tested the lock, but to no avail. She started through her entire set of picks again, jiggling each one to release the lock. Gowen's clock began to chime.

She reminded herself that in less than an hour, Gowen would arrive at his office. With renewed determination she began testing each pick a third time.

Over and over again, she thought she was disengaging the lock. Time and again, the door failed to open. She was about to give up when the image of Gaspar came to mind and she heard him say, *Thou shalt not give up!* She tried again, more carefully. This time, the door opened!

Ignoring the papers and ledger stacked on a shelf on the right, she set her hand and her mind to opening two locked drawers built inside the cubicle. Picking the lock on the upper one first, she pulled it out only to discover a stack of greenbacks. She shut it and focused on the lower drawer. She was sliding it open when she heard the unmistakable voices of Gowen and Clarissa Hackbardt as they came into the reception room.

CHAPTER 4

Heart pounding, Rosalie shut the drawer in Gowen's closet. She had lost all track of time, too involved in her task to heed the quarter-hour chimes of the clock. It was too late now to prevent him from finding her in his office. She grabbed a dust rag from her bucket, set to work polishing his already immaculate desk, and offered a smile when he came through the door.

"Good morning, Mr. Gowen! You're looking bright as a peacock's crest this morning!"

Despite her compliment, his expression grew dark and menacing. "You! What are you doing in my office?"

Clarissa entered the room, a look of pure revulsion in her eyes. "I'll tell you. She's been snooping! She's probably already searched every nook and cranny of your office!"

Rosalie drew herself up, squaring her shoulders as best she could. "I'm merely assisting Mrs. Potter with her cleaning, Miss Hackbardt. But I'm quite finished now." She dropped her rag into her bucket, picked it up, and headed for the door.

Gowen caught hold of her right arm. "Not so fast!"

His touch repulsed her. She twisted away and banged him on the shin with her bucket.

He cried out, letting go of her arm to grab his leg.

She hurried out the office door.

"Come back here!" he demanded, following her into the reception area. He caught hold of her bad shoulder. "You won't get away with this!" His thumb penetrated deeper as he spoke. "You'd better stay clear of this office from now on, or I'll see to it your aunt and uncle never work in this town again!"

Rosalie wanted to cry out from the pain of his cruel grip. Instead, she issued a warning. "You haven't seen the last of me yet, Mr. Gowen!"

She jerked free and hurried down the hall and out the door. All the way to the confectionery she dreaded having to tell her aunt and uncle that she'd come away empty-handed. To her amazement, neither of them asked the outcome of her search, but proceeded about their tasks as if the day had begun like any other. She put the entire cleaning escapade behind her as she helped her aunt with customers and her uncle with fudge-making— until an hour later when Kenton McCune came marching through the door and straight up to her.

"You broke your promise!" His accusation rang loud and clear in the small shop.

Two customers finishing their purchases turned to stare at them.

Rosalie stood mute. Warmth flooded her cheeks.

Lottie ushered the customers toward the door. "Thank you very much. Your patronage is greatly appreciated!"

She shut the door, hung up the "Closed" sign, pulled the shade, and turned to Kenton. "What promise are you talking about, Mr. McCune?"

Rosalie answered for him. "I went to Mr. Gowen's office after I gave Mr. McCune my word I'd stay away."

Kenton glowered at her. "That's right. And do you realize what you've done? You've made it ten times harder for me to solve the mortgage problem!"

"But I only wanted to—"

"It makes little difference what you *wanted* to do. What you *did* was make Gowen angry, retractable, and more determined than ever to put your aunt and uncle out of this shop at month's end!"

Ben spoke up. "Easy, Kenton. Anger won't solve the problem."

Kenton fumed under his breath.

Ben set down his fudge spatula and came to face him. "Rosalie was only trying to help. I'm not condoning her actions, but her heart was in the right place. Berating her will only make things worse."

Lottie went behind the display case, gathered some vanilla caramels into a box, and offered them to the lawyer. "Eat up, Mr. McCune. You've got to restore your old, sweet self before the ball tonight."

Kenton started to choke.

Rosalie came to his rescue. "No offense, Aunt Lottie, but you're not a fairy godmother, and Mr. McCune and I are a far piece from being Cinderella and the prince. I think we'd best cancel our plans for the ball."

Lottie scowled. "You're right. I'm *not* a fairy godmother, but I won't hear of your canceling! For days now, your uncle and I have been planning to buy tickets for the Opera House gallery so we can watch the two of you at the Carnival Queen's reception and dance."

"That's right," said Ben. "This is the first time in years I've consented to staying out past nine o'clock!"

"We're even skipping supper so we can cook the candy for tomorrow," Lottie said. "Goodness knows we won't feel like doing it at the crack of dawn." She paused, her gaze moving expectantly from Rosalie to Kenton. When silence reigned, she sighed deeply, heading to the door to remove the "Closed" sign.

Evidently guilt-ridden, Kenton took two tickets from his pocket and offered them to Ben. "Why don't you take your sister to the ball tonight?"

He laughed, then took out his handkerchief and wiped perspiration from his brow. "If you think I'm sweating now, it's nothing to what would happen if I had to dance at a ball."

Lottie joined them. "You just put those tickets back in your pocket, Mr. McCune. It's a shame they should go to waste, but I suppose there's nothing more to be done."

Customers entered the shop and Lottie started to wait on them while Ben went about slicing the latest batch of fudge.

Appearing contrite, Kenton approached Rosalie. "May I please speak with you outside for a moment?"

She nodded and led the way to the front sidewalk where he paused to face her.

"Miss Foxe, it's been said that the firmest friendships have been formed in mutual adversity."

She regarded him skeptically. "It's also been said that new friends, like one's best coat and patent leather boots, are only intended for holiday wear. At other times, they are neither serviceable nor at-all comfortable."

Kenton looked thoughtful. "Since this is a holiday, do you suppose you could find it in your heart to forgive my anger and accept my friendship—and my invitation—for the ball this evening?"

Following a pensive moment, she said, "I can on one condition—that you'll forgive me for breaking my word and going to Mr. Gowen's office when I promised I wouldn't. I was wrong."

He grinned. "It may be true that friendships are formed in mutual adversity, but they often owe longevity to mutual forgiveness. I'll come by for you at half-past nine."

He'd turned to go when Rosalie thought of a better idea. "Mr. McCune! Wait!"

He spun back around and his forehead wrinkled.

"Mr. McCune, why don't you come at half past eight? Then we can watch the Carnival Queen's parade from Aunt Lottie and Uncle Benjamin's front window."

A smile tilted his mustache. "I'll look forward to it!"

~~~

Heavy traffic in the confectionery made the day pass quickly for Rosalie. Guests were arriving in the city by the boatload and trainload for the Independence Day events, and it seemed they all needed to feed a sweet tooth. Work left her little time for private thought, but when she was alone in her room to prepare for the ball, she dropped to her knees beside her cot and folded her hands. "Dear Heavenly Father, I've sinned and need your forgiveness. I shouldn't have made a promise I meant to break, nor said things I didn't mean. Please help me to be more honest in the future. In Jesus' name, Amen." She started to rise, then added "And Lord, please let Uncle Benjamin, Aunt Lottie, Mr. McCune and me have an enjoyable evening."

She quickly gathered up her robe and headed upstairs to bathe, then returned to her room to don a fancy dress for the ball—one of creamy white satin. The bodice was accented by a lacy overlay that formed a high collar, then draped over her shoulders and dipped to a vee in front where it ended in a point at her wide belt. The skirt had a modest train consisting of eight rows of ruffles, and she felt positively regal when wearing it. A fine white cord beneath the train allowed her to lift it for dancing, and by looping it over her right wrist, she could partially hide the fact that she didn't have full use of her arm.

From her travel jewelry case she took the locket her aunt and uncle had sent her upon graduation from Salem Academy this past spring—a piece that had belonged to her maternal grandmother who had lived her entire life in Michigan and had died when Rosalie was a small child. As she admired the charm of the old gold against the lacy bodice of her dress, she realized it held more meaning now that she'd spent some time in her grandmother's home state.

She had put the finishing touches on her hair and found her gloves when she heard a knock and went to let Kenton in. As she opened the door, the din of the happy street crowd and strains of the band warming up for the start of the parade at the Opera House began to drift in. But she barely noticed them for the handsome figure standing before her.

Kenton looked well in everything from a baseball uniform to a morning suit, but she hadn't seen any man do such justice to a tailcoat and tie. He was holding a long-stemmed pink rose and hesitated a moment before offering it to her.

~~~

Kenton had anticipated the pleasing sight that would greet him when he saw Rosalie, but his expectations fell far short of the vision of loveliness being revealed to him now. He required a moment's thought to find the right words to accompany the rose.

"Miss Foxe, thou art fairer than the evening air clad in the beauty of a thousand stars. Forgive me for borrowing from Marlowe."

She gave a nervous laugh. "There's nothing at-all to forgive, Mr. McCune. I thank you for your borrowed words, and for this lovely blossom." When she had inhaled its sweet essence, she touched him lightly on the arm. "Come inside. From the sounds of things, the parade will be passing by any minute."

He willingly followed her upstairs to the apartment. In the sitting room, Ben had already arranged chairs by the windows overlooking Front Street, and Lottie had prepared a tray of small sandwiches and lemonade which she brought around as soon as Kenton and Rosalie were seated.

The street below, normally calm and dark on any other night, had been transformed by colored lights, red-fire flames, Japanese lanterns, and hordes of masked onlookers. The carnival atmosphere was heightened by the firing of Roman candles and sky rockets, and the approach of the first contingent of the parade, a band dressed in Rube costumes striking forth the patriotic strains of John Philip Sousa. Kenton relished the look of enjoyment on Rosalie's face as the notes of *Stars and Stripes Forever* sailed out, and her pure delight when cake walkers in funny, fetching costumes and a throng of bicycles bedecked in red, white, and blue streamers made an appearance.

The centerpiece of the procession followed—the queen's carriage decked out in colored flowers, its harness trimmed in white as it carried the carnival queen and her two ladies in waiting who had been chosen from many pretty contenders during several days of voting. Kenton watched them closely, a tad proud that his own horse, Judge, had been chosen from several offered to pull the carriage. He was thinking how regal his plumed gelding looked, prancing down the street, when Rosalie commented.

"You'd think they could have found a *white* horse for the queen's carriage."

Determined not to take offense, Kenton carefully explained. "Queen Edna had her choice of several horses, white ones included. She picked Judge."

Rosalie's cheeks grew as pink as the rose he'd given her. She offered no apology, but sipped her lemonade.

When the last unit in the parade, a military band, had passed by, Kenton said, "I think it's time we all stroll down to the Opera House and wait for the queen."

Lottie waved him off. "You two go on. Ben and I will be along as soon as I finish here." She picked up the refreshment tray and headed for the kitchen.

CHAPTER 5

A large crowd was pressing around the entrance to the Opera House when Rosalie arrived with Kenton. Thank goodness she wasn't given to claustrophobia. As had been announced in the newspaper, the queen and her court made a brief appearance there when the parade broke up, then they were driven to the Park Place Hotel for a rest while their guests were being admitted to the main floor and galleries of the Opera House.

Rosalie had also read in the paper that the queen expected all guests to remove their masks upon completion of the parade, and as some were complying with her wish, Kenton pointed out an exception.

"I see Mr. Gowen and his Miss Hackbardt are still in black masks." He held the Opera House door for Rosalie as she paused to glance over her shoulder.

"How can you be certain it's them?"

"You'll see. Now let's go inside."

Rosalie stepped into the main hall. It barely resembled a theater. Chairs had been removed and a hardwood dance floor installed. In addition, a throne had been set on the stage and draped with rich tapestries of silk in red, white, and blue.

A fourteen piece orchestra had been tucked into the pit below the stage and was playing overtures while the galleries filled with townsfolk. She spotted Benjamin and Lottie in the front row and from the way they waved to her, she could tell they were already enjoying themselves.

When the strains of *America* issued forth, the queen made her entrance to the hall. A hush fell over the crowd as two dignitaries led her across the floor.

When Queen Edna passed by, Rosalie couldn't help but admire the royal gown. The sleeves and yoke of the bodice were encrusted with silver spangles and pearls while the rest of the dress, with its pleated front and skirt, was fashioned of cream peau de soie. Over it, the queen was wearing a mantle of royal purple velvet with a cream satin lining and ermine trim. It was fastened with a fancy silver clasp that glimmered as brightly as the gilt crown atop her head.

Behind her were two little blond pages—a boy and a girl—holding her train. In their burgundy tights, velvet jackets, and caps, the children stole Rosalie's heart. Murmurs of affection echoed around them.

She nudged Kenton. "Have you ever seen anything so adorable?"

"From the sounds of it, most of us haven't."

The children were followed by the ladies in waiting, both wearing pink crepe de chine and silk. As they took their seats on either side of Queen Edna's throne, Rosalie caught a glimpse of a nearby couple still wearing black masks. They were indeed Miss Hackbardt and Mr. Gowen.

She tried to put them out of her mind as the prime minister of the evening, Mr. Thomas Bates, presented the queen.

"Ladies and gentlemen, her royal highness, Queen Edna!"

Enthusiastic applause, cheers, and whistles filled the air. After the queen took a gracious bow, the hall grew quiet again and Mr. Bates expressed words of welcome, concluding a few minutes later.

"The queen would like to extend her greetings to each of her honored guests in person, and will now leave the stage to move among you."

As the guests on the ballroom floor began parting to make room for the queen and her court, Clarissa and Mr. Gowen moved even closer to Rosalie than before.

Kenton grasped Rosalie's hand and whispered, "Let's find another place to stand."

Before they could ease away, Rosalie was accidentally pushed into Clarissa, causing the other woman's right shoe to come off.

Rosalie was instantly contrite. "I'm so sorry, Miss Hackbardt."

Clarissa snatched up her slipper. "You should watch where you're stepping!"

At the moment Clarissa slipped her foot into the satin shoe, Rosalie saw that a coin had been fastened inside the heel—a *gold* coin.

"Let me see that!" Rosalie demanded.

Clarissa scowled at her, then turned away.

Rosalie caught her by the arm. "You've hidden my double eagle inside your shoe!"

Clarissa wrenched free. "You're mad as a hatter, Miss Foxe, now leave me alone!"

Nearby guests began to whisper and stare.

Rosalie turned to Kenton. "She's got a gold coin in her right shoe. I saw it!"

Gowen pulled a candy from his pocket and offered it to Rosalie with a smile. "Have one of my butterscotch drops, Miss Foxe. It's guaranteed to chase away your delusions and put you in good humor."

Rosalie put palm out. "No offense, Mr. Gowen, but the day I eat one of your candies is the day—"

Kenton finished for her. "It's the day you find the coin you gave in payment for your aunt and uncle's store, isn't it, Miss Foxe?"

Cutler Gowen pulled off his mask, his smile vanishing. "Mr. McCune, Miss Foxe, your accusations about Miss Hackbardt and some twenty-dollar gold piece are getting tiresome." To Kenton, he said, "If your lady friend can't behave more civilly, take her home before she ruins the evening for the rest of us."

"I have a better idea." Kenton focused on Clarissa. "Why not simply take off your right shoe so we can all see whether or not you have Miss Foxe's double eagle?"

Before Clarissa could answer, Queen Edna approached Kenton accompanied by her entourage. "Mr. McCune, I'm so pleased you're here! I've been wanting to thank you in person for loaning your horse for the parade."

While Kenton's attention was on Queen Edna, Clarissa and Gowen slipped away. Releasing her hand from Kenton's, Rosalie started to follow, but several couples blocked her way. By the time she emerged from the throng, Clarissa and Gowen had disappeared. She hurried down the stairs and out onto the Front Street walk. They were but a few yards ahead of her. Half running, she caught up with Clarissa and stepped hard on her right heel.

"Ouch!" the woman cried, her slipper flying off.

Gowen started after it but Rosalie scooped it up before he could get a hand on it.

Clarissa hopped on her left foot, clutching her right heel with her gloved hand as she focused angrily on Rosalie. "Give me back my shoe!"

"Not until I see the coin!"

"I said, give me back my shoe!"

Unmindful of Clarissa's plea, Rosalie loosened the coin from the gum that was holding it in place and raised it to the light of the street lamp.

It was only a ten-dollar gold piece.

"I . . . I'm sorry," she said, warmth flooding her face as she handed the coin and the shoe to Clarissa.

Again, Gowen offered Rosalie a piece of candy. "You really ought to eat this butterscotch drop. It's guaranteed to turn a sour moment sweet." He pressed it into her empty hand and wrapped her fingers about it.

Still stunned with disappointment, Rosalie mumbled, "I . . . uh . . . excuse me." She backed away.

Having put on her shoe, Clarissa linked her arm with Gowen's. As the couple departed, Rosalie could tell

Gowen was quietly lecturing Clarissa but she couldn't make out the words. Desperate to know what was being said, she tucked the hard candy into her pocket and followed in the shadows of the buildings. Only some of his words were audible.

" . . . shoe is no place to keep your money . . . let me put it . . . "

As Gowen was speaking, Clarissa paused, looking over her shoulder.

Rosalie shrank back into the recessed doorway of Votruba's Harness Shop, distinctly hearing her say, "I think someone's following us."

Gowen clearly replied, "I don't see anyone. Come along, dear. We have our own private celebration to tend to. Tomorrow, the American Candy Company will be the talk of the town."

When their footsteps had receded, Rosalie peeked around the harness shop window. What had Gowen meant? Should she follow them or return to the ball?

A man's voice startled her.

"There you are, niece! We've been looking for you!"

She turned to face Uncle Benjamin.

Aunt Lottie stood beside him. "You worried us half to death, Rosalie!"

"I'm sorry, Aunt Lottie. I didn't mean to. I have something to tell you!" Rosalie linked her arms with theirs, words of explanation rolling off her tongue as they headed back toward the Opera House.

Moments later, Kenton found them and Rosalie repeated what she had told her relatives. She was finishing as the four of them reached the second floor of the hall.

"I just wish I knew what Mr. Gowen meant when he said the American Candy Company will be the talk of the town tomorrow."

Lilting strains of a Strauss waltz began to fill the air and Kenton offered Rosalie a smile. "I think we should forget about Mr. Gowen and enjoy the evening."

Lottie said, "By all means. I'm still waiting to see the two of you waltz."

Ben nudged Kenton toward the dance floor. "Go on, or I'll never hear the end of it."

He offered Rosalie his arm, and as she walked out onto the ballroom floor, she was determined to follow his advice—and his lead.

The limitations of her right shoulder and arm that had caused moments of awkwardness with dance partners in the past proved no obstacle to Kenton who simply placed both hands at her waist and stepped off in time to the music. He whisked her about the room as if they'd been dancing together for years. When he released his hold to twirl her around, he did so with such strength and elegance it was impossible for her to misstep. Other couples watched in awe, moving back to give them free reign of the dance floor. Even the queen and her court, who had moved to a settee in the corner of the dance floor to receive guests, had paused in their royal duties to look on in wonderment.

In Kenton's arms, time melted as swiftly as a spoonful of sugar in sassafras tea. When the last note of the last waltz had faded away, he walked her home behind Ben and Lottie who had stayed to watch every minute of the ball.

Ben paused at the bottom of the apartment stairs to consult his watch. "This is either the longest, or the shortest night I've ever known."

A firecracker sounded about a block away, prompting Lottie to comment. "It's the shortest—or will be if that noise keeps up. Good night Kenton. Good night, Rosalie."

She kissed her aunt and uncle on the cheek. "See you in the morning—*later* this morning, I mean."

When they had gone, she turned to Kenton. Even in the wan light of the street lamp he was more handsome than when he'd come to fetch her, for now they had shared a congenial evening and the effect was visible in his tender gaze, and in the smile beneath his mustache. But while her conscious thought was of this charming fellow with the glib tongue, a tiny corner of her mind wondered what new problems would surface for her aunt and uncle and their business on the morrow.

Kenton took both of Rosalie's hands in his and gazed tenderly upon her. The look in his eyes seemed to say that he no longer regarded her as the North Carolina miss he'd escorted to the ball as a favor to her aunt and uncle. Now that they'd traveled a mile of circles around the dance floor, could he possibly overlook her physical limitations? As he lifted her hands to his lips and brushed kisses against them, she silently thanked the Lord that she hadn't departed on the southbound train, praying that together they would soon solve the mystery of the missing mortgage payment.

The low roll of distant thunder interrupted her thoughts turning them to yet a different consideration. "I hope rain won't spoil the celebration tomorrow. You'll come and watch the parade with us if it's not canceled, won't you?"

"I'll come by tomorrow afternoon, rain or shine. Goodnight!"

No sooner had Kenton disappeared in the faint yellow haze of the street lights, than the image of Willy Jo flashed before her, bringing with it a twinge of guilt. How could she have so easily put her longtime neighbor friend from mind, never once thinking of him while dancing the night away with Kenton?

She closed and bolted the door against the increasing rumble of the approaching storm. In her room, she took her time putting away her formal gown, pausing to remove from her pocket the candy Gowen had given her. On a whim she popped the butterscotch drop into her mouth despite Kenton's prediction that she would not eat an American Candy Company candy until the day she had found the coin she had given in payment for the mortgage. Begrudgingly, she had to admit the butterscotch drop was as tasty as any of the hard candies her aunt and uncle produced.

As it melted on her tongue her thoughts shifted to the most pleasurable portion of the evening—the hours after midnight. Gowen seemed to be justified in claiming his candy could turn a sour moment sweet.

By the time she had donned her nightgown, brushed out her hair, and washed her face, thunder was cracking so loudly she knew she wouldn't be able to sleep. Taking from her trunk a pen, stationery, and a book for a lap desk, she propped herself against her pillows and started to pen a letter to her sister. With artful skill, she created lovely word pictures of Traverse City, made no mention of the problems regarding the mortgage, and included only a brief reference to Kenton McCune.

. . . Aunt Lottie, Uncle Benjamin, a lawyer friend of theirs, and I attended an Independence Day Ball this evening . . .

Long accustomed to the fact that Willy Jo wasn't the letter-writing kind and that communication between them was completely reliant on messages passed along by other family members, she included a note to him at the end.

P.S. Sometime when you're out riding, you might travel in the direction of the Winthrops and deliver my greetings to Willy Jo. Please tell him all is well with me here in the North Country and that I have thought of him often.

She resisted the urge to add *up until the last couple of days.*

With the worst of the storm over and the clock reading half past three in the morning, she set her letter, pen, and book aside and crawled between the sheets. Her sleep was intermittent, disturbed by further storms.

Rain continued throughout the morning causing cancellation of the bicycle races and Caledonian games that had been scheduled to start at nine, and all but eliminating customer traffic in the store. At noon the dark clouds began to clear, the sun peeked through, and word was passed along the street that the parade scheduled for one o'clock would begin on time.

But why didn't the candy store business improve with the weather and the increasing number of visitors mingling on the walks?

Kenton breezed through the door at a quarter past twelve. He wore his baseball uniform and a frown on his face. Had his game been canceled due to a flooded field? He wasted no time in revealing the real reason for his frown.

"Ben, Lottie, Miss Foxe, have you taken a look down Front Street since the weather cleared?" Met with silence and shrugs, he gravely advised, "You'd better come out here."

Rosalie shadowed him to the front walk. Her aunt and uncle followed close behind. Along the street, vendors had set up stands to hawk red lemonade, popcorn, roasted nuts, waffles, and fresh fruit, but these were not the object of his concern. Following the point of his finger, she discovered a cart about a block away gaily decorated with a red, white, and blue awning and skirt. Around it were gathered dozens of visitors. A huge sign explained the reason.

American Candy Co.
Free sweets!

Rosalie drew a sharp breath. "So *that's* why hardly anybody is coming into the store."

Ben shook his finger in the direction of the candy cart. "Gowen can't do that!"

Kenton said, "He can, and he is."

Lottie fussed with the neck strap of her apron. "We've got to do something!"

Ben grumbled. "What? Give away our fudge?"

Rosalie's mind spun. "Yes! We could give away little samples along with certificates enticing customers to come in and buy a pound of fudge and get a second pound free."

Ben shook his head. "I won't make a penny that way!"

"Maybe not," said Lottie, "but at least we'd be able to cover the cost of supplies. The way it looks now, our fudge will likely go stale before we can sell it all."

Kenton said, "I think your niece has the right idea."

Rosalie's heart pattered faster. "I'll decorate a basket in red, white, and blue streamers and fill it with the fudge cut into bite-size pieces. Aunt Lottie, you write out the certificates. Then, when the crowd gathers to watch the parade, I'll go up and down both sides of the street giving fudge and certificates to all who want them."

Lottie turned to go inside. "I'd better start writing."

CHAPTER 6

Three quarters of an hour later, with Kenton's help, Rosalie had purchased two egg baskets and yards of paper streamers from Wilhelm's Dry Goods. Soon, she had finished decorating and filling one of them with small pieces of vanilla and chocolate fudge—with and without walnuts—and dozens of certificates. Together, they began handing them out while Lottie and Ben prepared the second basket.

Busy as Rosalie was, she paused from time to time to watch the parade. The queen's barouche was one of the early entries, carrying the attractive young woman wearing a purple robe and gold crown. Despite Rosalie's feelings about grey geldings, she silently admitted that Judge looked smart drawing Miss Wilhelm's coach.

Following the royal carriage were two elaborate floats from the Catholic school. The first one carried a number of boys in costumes representing different nations with Uncle Sam in the center. Immediately behind it was another filled with dainty misses in picturesque national dress of many lands.

Not far behind, twelve-foot-high lumber wheels gaily trimmed with bunting showed what life in Caldwell and Lowdon's lumber woods might be on a holiday. Trailing it was a chariot covered by mirrors and gold paint. It carried the band of the Silver Brothers Show. Their teams of trained dogs and ponies followed, all in line.

Rosalie had turned her back to the procession to hand out more samples when Kenton tapped her shoulder. "You'd better take a look."

He pointed to a wagon that had been dressed with a bunting of patriotic colors and topped with a red and white *sign—AMERICAN CANDY CO. QUEEN.* Beneath it on a throne covered with blue paper flowers sat Clarissa Hackbardt in a white dress and flaming red cloak. A crown of silver topped her head. At her feet were mounds of wrapped candy which she tossed by the handfuls into the crowd.

Children rushed past Rosalie to fetch the treats, knocking the basket out of her hand and pushing her off balance. Kenton caught her about the waist, preventing her from falling, but he couldn't keep the fudge from flying into the dirt and the certificates from scattering across the street, only to land beneath the wheels of Clarissa's float.

The Candy Queen smiled fiendishly at Rosalie's plight.

The act set Rosalie's blood boiling and she clamped her jaw shut to silence the unladylike reprisal on her tongue.

"Never mind her," said Kenton, stooping to gather up the ruined goods. "I'll go and see if the other basket is ready."

Rosalie tried to focus on the parade but angry thoughts prevented her from appreciating the dainty white swan cart of the Traverse City Wagon Works and the examples of their wagons rolling along behind. Even a horseless electric carriage advertising Steinberg's Grand with the legend, *Traverse City and Old Mission R'y,* didn't amuse her, though all around her, folks were laughing.

Kenton returned with the new basket as the automobile rolled by. Together, they were able to pass out most of the fudge and certificates before the parade came to an end.

When the crowd broke up, he said, "I'll come by at half past eight to go with you to the fireworks. I've got to get to the baseball field now."

She bid him good bye and returned to the confectionery, pleased to see that with the parade over, customers were starting to redeem the certificates she and Kenton had given away. In mid-afternoon a young blond girl of about thirteen dressed in a riding helmet, jodhpurs, and boots, came into the store. The sight of her sparked thoughts of Vanda Mae. For a moment, Rosalie wondered how her horse-crazy younger sister was spending Independence Day.

The press of customers quickly brought Rosalie's thoughts back to the job at hand. She helped her aunt behind the candy counter a few minutes longer until a band struck up a concert in the street outside the shop.

Lottie nudged her toward the door. "Go on out there and listen. It's time you took a break." Shoving a penny into her hand, she added, "And treat yourself to some red lemonade. You deserve it!"

Rosalie went willingly, thankful for the cooling effect of the lemonade and the break from the close air indoors. The band—Harrington's Band according to the banner it displayed—was better than most. She thoroughly enjoyed their concert of patriotic tunes. *The Star Spangled Banner, America,* and *Yankee Doodle* topped their program, but she couldn't believe her ears when the conductor lit into a rousing rendition of *Marching Through Georgia.*

Every fiber of her being tensed. Unmindful of anything but the indignation simmering inside, she stormed into the confectionery.

"I hate this place!"

Lottie turned to her with alarm.

A woman customer swung around to face her. "I beg your pardon, young lady?"

Instantly regretful, Rosalie choked out the words, "Nothing . . . nothing at-all."

She ran through the shop to her room at the back, shut and bolted herself inside, and leaned against the door.

A wave of homesickness swept over her drowning her in a sea of self-pity. Hearing that Yankee song seemed to bring the troubles of the past few days to a head. Tears began to roll down her cheeks. She buried her face in her apron and slumped to the floor, muttering as she sobbed. "I wish I . . . were back in North Carolina . . . in the mountains. Oh, Mama, how I miss you!"

A knock sounded quietly on her door, then Lottie spoke, her voice laden with concern. "Rosalie, are you all right, dear?"

Her sympathetic tone only made Rosalie cry harder.

Lottie jiggled the door handle. "Let me in, dear."

Rosalie dabbed her eyes and got to her feet, still unable to stop crying and unwilling to obey.

Her aunt knocked again. *"Please* let me in or I'll have to ask Ben to take your door off the hinges."

After drying her cheeks and blowing her nose into her handkerchief, she unlocked the door.

Lottie enfolded her in a soft, warm hug and for a moment Rosalie imagined she was home in Shani's arms. The realization that Shani was hundreds of miles away caused new tears to leak out.

Her aunt released her, drying Rosalie's cheeks with the corner of her own apron. "What's troubling you, child? Surely it can't be as bad as all this."

Rosalie cleared her throat, replying in a shaky voice. "Did you hear . . . that awful song the band played?"

Lottie shook her head. "What song would that be, dear?"

Rosalie drew a deep breath. *"Marching Through Georgia.* Imagine them playing such a piece on the Fourth of July!"

"No offense was intended."

Rosalie turned away, pacing to the other end of her small room. Faintly, in the distance, she could hear the strains of *Battle Hymn of the Republic.* She pressed her hands over her ears.

Lottie left her, returning moments later when the song had ended. "Come with me, now. There's something I want you to hear." Taking her by the hand, she led Rosalie through the store and out onto the walk.

The band conductor looked at her and smiled, then turned to his musicians, raised his baton and struck up *Dixie,* following it immediately with a sentimental rendition of *Way Down Upon the Swanee River.*

Rosalie wanted to cry again, but she managed to keep back her tears. When the concert had ended and she returned to the empty store, she pondered the troubles still facing her aunt and uncle over their mortgage. Into her mind flowed one compelling thought.

No matter how much I miss North Carolina, I won't leave Michigan until I find the coin Clarissa stole!

~~~

Nearly three weeks later, on a Sunday morning, Rosalie awoke with soreness in her good shoulder. After setting aside the Joseph Conrad novel she'd been reading when she'd fallen asleep, she rotated her shoulder slowly to loosen the tense muscles, muttering to herself. "That's what I get for carrying a basket full of fudge to the dock three times a day. It's a good thing it's helping some, too. The way Gowen is operating, hardly anybody would bother coming up to the store if I didn't bribe them with certificates for free fudge."

From the Fourth of July on, she'd seen the American Candy Company carts every day outside the depot and parked by the dock where hundreds of passengers came off the steamers. With their awnings and skirts of red, white, and blue, they stole customers from her aunt and uncle. In an effort to keep patrons frequenting their store, Rosalie had continued to hand out samples of fudge and certificates for a free pound with each pound purchased from the candy shop.

With the continued competition and the necessity for discounts, income was barely keeping pace with expenses, but as she dressed for breakfast, she said a prayer of thanks that for now, the business was surviving. Later, when she sat down to pancakes and bacon with her Aunt Lottie and Uncle Benjamin, other problems occupied her mind—frustration over her inability to locate the nicked double eagle and anxiety over what would become of her aunt and uncle at month's end.

Curiosity was eating Rosalie up inside over the fragment of conversation she'd overheard between Mr. Gowen and Clarissa Hackbardt. She felt it was leading her to make another visit to Cutler Gowen's office to search the drawer she'd been unable to investigate; but she hadn't dared brave another early morning venture there after the trouble encountered on the first visit. And no reasonable possibilities had come to mind for further investigation of Clarissa. According to the Doyle sisters, she had taken a room near Cutler Gowen's home on Sixth Street. She had probably rid herself of the coin long ago.

As for Kenton McCune, Rosalie had seen him only on the rides he had provided to and from St. Francis Church on Sundays. At those times he had reported no progress forestalling the foreclosure on the mortgage. When Rosalie had criticized him for not taking a stronger stand with Cutler Gowen, her aunt and uncle had skillfully diverted conversation to another topic. In the privacy of the apartment, they refused to discuss the issue with her, preferring to pretend nothing at-all was amiss.

But Rosalie could no longer pretend the problem didn't exist. Swallowing the last of her pancakes, she set down her fork and pinned her gaze on her kin.

"Aunt Lottie, Uncle Benjamin, today is the twenty-second of July. Do you realize that in a little more than a week, Mr. Gowen is going to toss us out of here, like bad pennies to a pauper?"

Ben folded his napkin and laid it aside. "How can he? He must know you made the payment. Certainly, the man's got conscience enough to—"

Rosalie interrupted. "Uncle Benjamin, don't you understand? That man is so low, he could walk under a trundle bed with his top hat on!"

Ben smiled. "I can't believe that, but even if he *is* as bad as you believe, he could suffer a change of heart. The Lord can work miracles, you know." He stacked his plate on Lottie's, carried them to the sink, and began filling the dish pan with water.

Lottie spoke as she slipped napkins back into their rings. "That's right, dear. The Lord will provide."

Rosalie took her dirty plate to the sink. "You two sound just like Mama. She's always saying those things." Picking up the dish rag, she wiped drops of maple syrup from the table, then turned again to her aunt and uncle. "But there's something else she says, too."

Lottie adjusted the neck strap on her apron as she focused on Rosalie.

Ben turned to face her, wiping the dish soap from his hands and pushing up his glasses.

Rosalie continued. "Mama says the Lord helps those who help themselves."

Ben wrapped his arm about her waist. "We know, niece. And we know, too, that the three of us—and Mr. McCune—have done everything humanly possible to solve our problem with Mr. Gowen. Now, it truly *is* in the Lord's hands."

CHAPTER 7

Sunday morning, a week later, as Rosalie climbed the stairs that led from her bedroom behind the candy shop to the apartment above, she couldn't help feeling low. The candy business was off more than ever. Only two days remained until Cutler Gowen would repossess the building. Worst of all, her aunt and uncle had fallen into almost total silence.

She hoped things would improve before Mr. McCune picked them up for church. Last night he'd rung up to invite all three of them to join him for Sunday dinner after services, promising to take them to a special, undisclosed location. Rosalie prayed her aunt's and her uncle's sour moods wouldn't spoil the affair, even though she herself wanted more than ever to scold their lawyer friend for his inaction regarding Cutler Gowen. But when she had expressed such sentiments to Benjamin and Lottie last evening, they had made her promise she wouldn't mention the subject today.

As she opened the apartment door, a hint of fresh coffee and pancakes hot off the griddle greeted her. Despite the enticing aromas, she paused in the small parlor. Her uncle was finally talking again—more loudly than usual. The anger in his voice caught her by surprise.

"I told you not to send the girl to Gowen's office with the payment in the first place, but you didn't listen. You never listen."

Rosalie knew she should step into the kitchen, but instead she remained frozen in place.

Lottie responded calmly. "I wonder where Kenton is taking us for dinner today."

Ben went on. "We should have let Rosalie go home when she wanted, but you insisted on sending Kenton after her."

Lottie spoke again. "I'm glad of it, too. They got along so beautifully on the evening of the ball, it's a shame they haven't seen one another socially since. I'm glad they'll be together for dinner this afternoon."

Rosalie was about to make her presence known, but her uncle's heated words prevented her.

"Don't you understand? Rosalie's miserable here because of all our troubles—and weary from carrying that candy basket to the dock every day. But you haven't even noticed!"

A silent moment lapsed, then Lottie replied evenly, "I have too noticed, just like I'm noticing you, now. And what I'm hearing, Ben, is that after four weeks of telling us it's all in God's hands—after a month of claiming we've done everything possible to solve our problems with Mr. Gowen—you're scared to death we're really going to lose this place."

Rosalie didn't wait for her uncle's reply. Carrying her shoulders as erect as she could, she marched into the kitchen, a smile on her face. "Good morning Aunt Lottie, good morning Uncle Benjamin!" She kissed each of them on the cheek.

They bid her good morning, then her uncle started to get up to hold her chair.

She put a staying hand on his shoulder and seated herself. "Uncle Benjamin, it's evident to me that you're about as discouraged as a rice planter up a salt river right now."

He almost smiled.

She went on. "And there's something else I couldn't help noticing, too." She gestured toward the open kitchen window. "The sun's bright as angel's eyes. The sky is blue like the sea of a dream—"

Ben pushed up his glasses. "You've been reading Joseph Conrad—that part about the sea."

Rosalie chuckled. Her uncle had been suggesting she read his favorite author since she'd first arrived in Traverse City and she'd only done so in the past couple of days. "Yes, I've been reading Mr. Conrad's stories. And you know what I think he'd tell you if he were here right now?"

Ben regarded her with interest.

"He'd say a foul wind may be astir, and a tempest may be brewing, but what you've got right now is the calm before the storm, and you might as well enjoy it till it's time to batten down the hatches."

Lottie took a platter of pancakes from the warming oven and passed them to her brother. "The girl's right,

Ben. Now let's eat. Mr. McCune will be here before you know it."

~~~

When services had ended at St. Francis Church, Kenton helped Rosalie into the front seat of his rig while Ben and Lottie settled in the back. As the carriage rolled along Cass toward the bay, Rosalie fingered the lace on her collar. The infrequent conversations between her and Kenton since the Carnival Ball had been contentious. Could they be otherwise now?

He turned to her and drew a deep breath. "Do I detect the fragrance of peach blossoms?"

Rosalie grinned. "I plead guilty."

A smile tipped the corners of his mouth. "Lovely as the young miss who wears it." His gaze lingered on her, as if taking in the ivory lace collar and pink satin ribbon she'd so carefully added to her plain shirtwaist this morning.

She observed him openly. He cut a fine figure with his tall silk hat, perfectly trimmed mustache and beard, gray frock coat, and pinstripe pants. He'd been going to some trouble, too, hiring a chestnut mare each Sunday to pull his rig, rather than hitching up his own grey gelding. She couldn't help liking him for it, even if she was still piqued that he was letting Gowen get the best of her aunt and uncle without seeming to lift a hand to help out.

But today, she would follow her own advice and appreciate the calm before the storm, pushing the mortgage problem to the back of her mind to enjoy Kenton's company. Despite the considerable difference in their ages—and opinions—she now realized he was easier to like than she had given him credit for. As Kenton turned onto Washington Street, she prayed his special dinner plans would go smoothly.

He slowed down near the Doyle sisters' home. "Why didn't you tell us you were taking us to visit Miss Ava and Miss Eda for dinner? It'll be a real pleasure to see those ladies again."

Lottie spoke up from the back seat. "Yes, Kenton, why didn't you tell us? I'd have brought a box of those Jordan almonds the Doyle sisters like so well. Lord knows we've got plenty, business being what it is."

Kenton remained silent until he'd passed the spinster ladies' drive and pulled into the one belonging to the house just beyond. "As you can see, we're not exactly going to the Doyles', although they will be joining us for dinner."

"Whose place is this?" Rosalie wanted to know.

"I don't believe any customers of ours live here," said Lottie. "I know all the local folks who come into the shop."

"I thought this house was for sale," said Ben.

Kenton turned to him with a grin. "It was."

"I think a lawyer must have bought the place," said Rosalie, "a lawyer with a real fondness for vanilla caramels."

Aunt Lottie leaned forward. "Kenton, is it true? Did *you* buy this house?"

The Doyle sisters emerged on the porch and Miss Eda called to them, beckoning with her lace handkerchief. "Welcome to Mr. McCune's new home!"

"Come right in!" said Ava. "There's just time enough to tour the house before dinner."

Ben helped Lottie down while Kenton did the same for Rosalie. As they followed the walk to the porch, she gave the place a good looking-over. Neither modest nor a mansion, it rose three stories high and included a veranda along the front and east sides, a second story balcony containing a hammock, and a pretty little eyebrow window cut into the slope of the slate roof above. Window trim of sienna and bright yellow contrasted nicely with the muted beige-pink tone of the clapboard siding.

"This place is lovely, Kenton," said Lottie, "but I thought you were happy in your old one."

"I was, but I decided it was time for a change, and this house caught my eye." Climbing the steps to the porch where the Doyles were waiting for them, he added, "Besides, I couldn't ask for nicer neighbors."

Ava Doyle greeted them cordially. "Isn't it wonderful Mr. McCune is living next to us now?"

"We'll have so many more opportunities to beat—I mean play him in euchre," said Eda. "Maybe we can get up a game after dinner. I've brought my lucky deck—"

Ava interrupted. "Hush sister, and see these folks inside."

Rosalie entered through oak double doors, left her hat and gloves on the hall tree in the vestibule, then proceeded with the others through a wide hall to a parlor on the left. The front bay window and two side windows allowed ample daylight through Battenberg lace curtains to enhance the mahogany wainscoting and the forest green velvet on the sofa and love seat.

Across one corner of the room stood a spinet piano. "Do you play, Mr. McCune?" Rosalie asked.

Before he could answer, Ava said, "You should hear him. He could be a concert soloist."

Rosalie lifted the piano lid. "Then surely, Mr. McCune, you'll play a tune to put us in the mood for dinner."

Kenton shook his head. "I'd much rather hear—" He stopped himself short. Color invaded his cheeks.

Using her left hand, Rosalie quickly played the melody to the words, "While strolling in the park one day, all in the merry month of May."

Kenton's eyes widened.

Rosalie smiled. "My sister and I play piano together quite often when we're both at Tanglewood. I'll play with you now, if you like."

Kenton pulled out the piano bench for her and motioned to his other guests. "Gather 'round. There's time for a verse of *A Fountain in the Park* before Mrs. Buckley—my hired woman—serves dinner."

Ava and Eda sang surprisingly good harmony while Ben sang the melody an octave lower and Lottie sang quietly off-key.

When they had finished, a woman in a grey dress, white apron, and mobcap was standing at the parlor door.

"Dinner is ready, sir," she told Kenton.

"Thank you, Mrs. Buckley." He closed the piano lid and turned to Rosalie. I hope you'll play another song with me after dinner."

"Certainly—*after* you show us the rest of your house."

He smiled. "I'm sure that can be arranged."

~~~

Rosalie had eaten her fill of Mrs. Buckley's planked trout and freshly picked corn and was savoring the last bite of her peach cobbler when Kenton said, "I'd really like to play another song with you at the piano, Miss Foxe."

"You promised to show us the house first, remember?"

He smiled. "Then let's finish the tour." He rose to hold her chair. The others rose, also.

Ava stepped past Kenton. "Mr. McCune, the first thing you must show your friends is the wonderful sleeping chamber you've made for yourself out of the reception room." She led the way to a closed pocket door left of the entry.

Kenton paused, his hand on the door panel, and Rosalie sensed his reluctance to expose his private quarters. She was on the brink of suggesting they skip this room when he slid the door open wide.

Behind it, a heavily carved bed with high posters and a crewel embroidered canopy dominated a room divided by a tapestry dressing screen. On the opposite side of the screen—a scene of a fox chasing a hound—was a corner study made cozy by a leather winged chair, a case full of books, and a table covered with a cluster of photographs.

"See? Isn't it stately?" Ava asked.

Rosalie nodded. "Very handsome."

She was about to inquire about the portraits when Kenton slid the door shut. "The rooms I really want you to see are on the second floor. I'll show you."

Upstairs, the decor was much lighter. The Doyle sisters displayed a remarkable talent for pointing out the best features of each of the three bedrooms. One had its own fireplace and bay window and reminded Rosalie very much of her own bedroom at Tanglewood with its sheer Priscilla curtains and soft, pink window seat cushion. The second of the bedrooms was slightly smaller with a lavender canopy on its double bed, while the third sleeping chamber was decorated in browns, russets, and golds pleasing to any man.

Touching Rosalie's elbow, Ava said, "Wait until you see what Mr. McCune has put in at the end of the hall."

Fussing with her lace handkerchief, Eda added, "It's just the cutest thing. I wish we had the same in our place."

As Rosalie followed the ladies toward the back of the house, she was faintly aware of someone ringing the front doorbell. Who had come to call? Her silent question was forgotten when she turned the corner to find a small kitchen and eating area complete with a little stove, ice box, sink, and table.

Lottie spoke to Kenton as she gazed about the small, but efficient kitchen. "This floor is set up as an apartment. Are you thinking of renting it out?"

Kenton shifted his weight. He seemed on the verge of answering when Mrs. Buckley came up the stairs calling his name. "Excuse me, please. I'll be right back."

While the Doyle sisters discussed the tidy arrangement of the kitchen with Lottie, Rosalie eased away. Her uncle did the same.

Despite Mrs. Buckley's hushed tone, Rosalie caught the words, "Mr. Gowen is here."

Kenton replied, "Tell him we'll be right down."

When Rosalie's gaze met her uncle's, there was no mistaking the pent-up resentment, indignation, and anger waiting to burst forth.

CHAPTER 8

Kenton turned to Rosalie and Ben, apprehension written in the crease between his brows. "Someone is here to see—"

Ben interrupted. "It's Gowen. I heard. I'm going down and have a word with him." He headed for the stairs.

Kenton stopped him, his hand on Ben's shoulder. "Please. Let me handle it."

Ben pulled away. "I've let you handle it up till now and things have only gotten worse. It's my turn."

Lottie emerged from the kitchen alcove, Ava and Eda right behind. "What is it, Ben?"

"Gowen's downstairs."

Ava blinked rapidly. "Mr. Gowen? Here?"

Eda addressed Kenton, her handkerchief aflutter. "I can't believe he'd darken your door."

Kenton's brow quirked. "You might be surprised—"

Ben headed toward the stairs. "Gowen's the one in for a surprise. He evidently thinks I'm as soft and sweet as my fudge, and just as easily done away with. It's time he learned different."

Lottie followed her brother. "That's right. It's time he learned we Marshalls can't be pushed around like a batch of warm fudge on a slab of marble."

Ava followed Lottie. "I'd like to bend Mr. Gowen's ear myself."

Eda trailed the others. "I'm with you, sister."

Kenton started after them. "Folks, please. It's not what—"

Rosalie caught Kenton by the elbow. "For weeks we've been waiting for you to solve our problems with Gowen. Now Aunt Lottie and Uncle Benjamin are all but out of business. We deserve our say with that scalawag and there's nothing you can do to stop us!" She hurried past him.

Kenton started after her. "I'm telling you, it's not what you think!"

Rosalie ignored him, following the charge into the parlor.

Gowen rose from the dark green velvet love seat the moment her uncle stepped into the room. "Good afternoon—"

Ben cut him off. "Don't you 'good-afternoon' me, you—"

Lottie interrupted, "deceitful, conniving—."

Ava took up the assault, "—immoral, indecent—"

Eda chimed in. "—unethical, unscrupulous—"

Ava continued, "—venal, vile person. What do you mean, cheating these decent, hardworking folks?"

"Yes, what do you mean, Mr. Gowen?" Eda asked.

Rosalie spoke up. "You ought to be ashamed of yourself, Mr. Gowen, *mighty* ashamed, cheating my Aunt Lottie and Uncle Benjamin out of what's rightfully theirs."

Ben's cheeks flushed, his jaws drawn taut as he shook his fist in Gowen's face. "If you think you can just turn me out of my store like lollipops from a mold, you've got another thing coming. I plan to fight till my dying breath for what's mine, the consequences be—"

Gowen cut in. "The consequences might be to your liking, Mr. Marshall. You're practically out of business, anyway. I came to offer a proposal I'm sure will satisfy you and your sister."

Ben pushed up his glasses. "The only thing that will satisfy me is the sight of you ripping up that eviction notice."

Gowen regarded him skeptically. "The *only* thing?"

"The *only* thing!"

"That's a real shame, Mr. Marshall, because I came here with a better idea."

"Don't waste your breath."

"You ought to at least hear me out. Mr. McCune has spent a tremendous amount of time petitioning me on your behalf. Even *he* thought you'd like my proposition."

Ben turned to Kenton. "Is that true?"

Kenton shifted his weight. "Mr. Gowen is determined to foreclose on the property you now occupy, but Ben, as long as the American Candy Company is around, your business there won't ever be what it was. Mr. Gowen has a good offer if you'll only hear him out."

Ben regarded Gowen skeptically.

Indicating the love seat, Gowen said, "Why don't you and your sister sit? We'll talk."

As Ben and Lottie settled on the love seat, Ava nudged Eda toward the sofa. "I want to hear what Mr. Gowen has to say. Don't you, sister?"

Eda dabbed her temples with her handkerchief. "I most certainly do."

Kenton offered Rosalie a chair near Ben and Lottie, then took one beside her, leaving the large chair opposite them for Gowen.

He sat, focusing his dark eyes on Ben. "Mr. Marshall, you're the best confectioner in all of Northern Michigan, American Candy Company *not* excepted. In fact, I'd like very much for you—and your sister—to come to work for me.

Ben smiled cynically. "Work for you? Never!"

Gowen reached for his inside jacket pocket, producing a folded paper. "I'm willing to give you an excellent salary—far above what you were making even when your business was brisk." He offered Ben the document.

Ben hesitated, then opened it for both he and Lottie to read. Seconds later he looked up, his eyes wide. "It says here that in addition to guaranteed employment and generous salaries, you want to buy our fudge recipe for . . ." He pointed to a figure on the page, turning it for Gowen to see. "Is this amount correct?"

Gowen glanced at the number. "That's right. But if you don't think it's fair, I'm willing to—"

Ben shook his head. "It's *not* fair—at least not to you. But if you want to pay too much, I won't refuse your money." He turned to Lottie. "Will you?"

She focused on the page, then on Gowen, a speculative look in her eyes. "This is all well and good as far as it goes, but where are we to live once you've put us out of our apartment?"

Rosalie spoke up. "Yes, where *are* we to live, Mr. Gowen? And what about the money Uncle Benjamin and Aunt Lottie have already paid for that building?"

Kenton cleared his throat. "That's been a point of considerable discussion between Mr. Gowen and me."

Gowen explained. "If you're willing to move into the apartment upstairs here, I'll apply all the equity you have in the Queen City Candy Shoppe to this house, making you co-owners with Mr. McCune."

Kenton said, "If this place isn't to your liking, Mr. Gowen has agreed to apply the equity to a more suitable property."

Gowen grinned. "I own a choice little house closer to the candy factory."

Ben shook his head vigorously. "This place is fine, don't you think, Lottie?"

She smiled. "It's more than fine. It's perfect!"

Ben turned to Gowen. "The move will be expensive. With business off, we're strapped for cash money."

Lottie added, "And there's all the candy supplies and equipment to sell."

"I'll buy them at top prices," said Gowen, "and I'll provide men and a wagon to move your household goods as soon as you're ready—at no cost to you."

Ben pounded his fist against the arm of the love seat. "You've been planning this for months, probably since the day you took over the mortgage from Mr. Newton, haven't you? Just waiting for the time when you could force us out of the candy shop and move right in. You're nothing but a . . . a . . . ."

Gowen put up his hand. "You seem to forget. You defaulted on the mortgage payment."

Ben's face colored deeply. "I did *not!*"

"Then prove it!"

Kenton spoke up. "Gentlemen, there's no point in going over old ground. Ben, I'm sorry, but Mr. Gowen's proposals are the best I can do for you."

Lottie touched Ben's arm. "Accept the offer. We'll have good pay, a nice home . . ."

"And us for neighbors," said Ava.

"Yes, and a euchre game anytime you want," said Eda.

When Ben remained silent, Gowen said, "Maybe you need a day to think about it." He started to rise.

Ben put palm out. "No. We'll be ready for your movers come Wednesday morning, and the Monday following, Lottie and I will report to your factory for work."

Gowen nodded. "I'll write a draft to Mr. McCune for your share of this house first thing tomorrow."

"And be sure to provide Uncle Benjamin with a written statement regarding the transfer of funds," said Rosalie. "We want no question this time."

Gowen said, "I guarantee there will be no problems, Miss Foxe."

"I'll personally see that the papers are in order," said Kenton, "including a purchase agreement on this place regarding Ben and Lottie's share in it."

While he was seeing Gowen to the door, Miss Ava focused on Ben. "You won't regret moving to this neighborhood."

"We'll be glad to entertain your niece while you and your sister are at the candy factory," said Miss Eda.

Rosalie quickly reassessed her private vow to remain in Michigan until she had found the coin Clarissa had stolen. "That won't be necessary, Miss Eda. Now that Mr. Gowen has offered fair settlement to Uncle Benjamin and Aunt Lottie, it's time I went home to North Carolina."

Kenton joined them again as she finished speaking. "Miss Foxe, I wonder if you'd consider remaining in Michigan awhile longer. The fellow who was assisting me at my office has resigned for a better position downstate, and I could use the help of a well-educated young woman, preferably one from North Carolina."

Lottie said, "There's an extra bedroom upstairs here for you to stay in."

Ben nodded. "And far more comfortable than that tiny one you're in behind the shop."

Ava blinked rapidly. "I think you're meant to stay in Traverse City awhile, Miss Foxe."

Eda fussed with her handkerchief. "Maybe Mr. McCune will let you off work early once in a while. It would be nice if we could get in a game or two of euchre before you head south."

"You could start at my office next Monday," said Kenton. "That will give you a few days to settle in here. I usually work from nine until six, but you could work whatever hours you wish."

Rosalie was about to accept Kenton's offer when a tiny voice inside prompted her to make a minor change. "Mr. McCune, I'll come to work for you, nine to six, but I'd prefer to start this Thursday morning instead of next Monday. One day is sufficient to move my meager belongings."

Kenton beamed. "Excellent!"

When his smile quickly faded, Rosalie said, "Something troubling you, Mr. McCune?"

"Just a minor complication." Smiling again, he said, "I'm really pleased you've agreed to help me."

"I look forward to it," she assured him. To Ben and Lottie, she said, "I'd better write to my folks tonight about the change in our address—*and* in our employment."

~~~

On the following Wednesday afternoon as Rosalie unpacked her trunk in her new bedroom, gratefulness washed over her. Her aunt and uncle owned a substantial share of this lovely home with papers to prove it, the move from the tiny apartment couldn't have gone smoother, and they would soon be paid better than ever for doing what they loved most—making candy. But certain situations remained a puzzle to her regarding Cutler

Gowen's dealings. She must ask Kenton about them when he returned from his law office at the end of the day.

At about four-thirty when she was helping her aunt unpack her clothes, Mrs. Buckley called Lottie to the downstairs phone. Rosalie thought nothing of it when her aunt said it was only Kenton checking on dinner plans.

But he arrived home shortly thereafter—almost two hours earlier than Rosalie had expected. And from the front window of her aunt's bedroom, she saw that instead of driving straight into the carriage house with Judge, he parked by the curb. A cab drawn by a chestnut Thoroughbred pulled to a halt right behind him. Kenton spoke to the driver, then headed toward the house. When she mentioned the curious situation to her aunt, Lottie nudged her out the bedroom door.

"You'd better go down and see what's on Kenton's mind." She offered a curious smile.

Rosalie hurried downstairs, meeting up with him as he came through the door.

His hazel-come-grey eyes were twinkling. "Miss Foxe, come with me. We're going for an afternoon drive."

He held the door for her but she hesitated. "Hadn't I better tell Aunt Lottie—"

"She already knows where I'm taking you. It's just outside of town. Now come." He nudged her elbow. On the way down the front walk, he explained further. "If we're going to ride together to my office every day, I've got to find a horse you trust. I want you to pick one you'd be comfortable with."

Kenton handed her into the cab and instructed the driver to follow him as he drove Judge and his own rig. Ten minutes later he turned at the entrance to a horse farm set back off the road. The front pasture, picturesque with pond and whitewashed fence, held two mares with their foals. Behind it were other pastures holding from three to five horses apiece in a wide range of colors and breeds.

The drive ended at a stable. To the right stood a tall white farmhouse dripping with carpenter's lace. To the left of the stable was a riding ring. A girl of about thirteen was putting a dun-colored mare through her paces. Her fair hair was caught back in a blue ribbon that streamed down her back beneath her riding helmet. Rosalie couldn't help remembering herself at a slightly younger age atop Hurricane, poised and confident in the saddle.

When the young girl caught sight of Kenton, she quickly left the riding ring and hitched her horse to the fence post. Climbing to the top rail, she waved enthusiastically to Kenton, her face beaming.

"Hello, Mr. McCune! Papa's in the stable. I'll fetch him." She jumped down from the fence and hurried off, her progress impeded by a slight limp.

A moment later she emerged alongside a tall blond fellow wearing leather leggings. When he had greeted Kenton with a handshake, the three of them approached the hired rig. Kenton gave Rosalie a hand down, introducing her.

"Miss Foxe, I'd like you to meet some friends of mine, Miss Susan Reddick and her father, Mr. John Reddick, a renowned horse breeder and trainer in these parts."

The young girl looked vaguely familiar but Rosalie couldn't think why. She inferred from Susan's scrutinizing gaze and the looks of admiration sent Kenton's way that the two of them were longtime friends. She offered her hand to the girl and her father in turn. In the slump to Mr. Reddick's shoulders and the lack of conviction in his handshake, she sensed a weariness that no single good night's sleep could cure.

To John, Kenton said, "I'd like you to show Miss Foxe your most trustworthy driving horses—in any color but grey."

John's broad smile spread all the way to his blue eyes, partially erasing the tiredness evident there as well. "Come with me. I've brought in a couple of horses that I think will serve your purpose."

Rosalie made conversation with the Reddick girl as they followed the men to the stable.

"Have you ever been to the confectionery in town? I used to work there, and you look familiar."

Susan appeared thoughtful. "I was there to buy fudge on the Fourth of July. We got a pound free . . . but I don't remember seeing you there. An older woman waited on me.

Rosalie remembered then, Susan had been in the shop shortly before the band had struck up their sidewalk concert—and a bad case of homesickness. Pushing unhappy memories aside, Rosalie quickly changed topics.

"How long have you been riding? I couldn't help but admire your form."

Susan smiled. "Since I was three. Papa used to set me on the saddle right in front of him."

Rosalie chuckled. "I have pictures of myself at that age with my daddy on his horse, and others with my mama on her horse as well." She sighed. "An ocean's-worth of water has gone down the Yadkin since then." At Susan's puzzled look, she explained, "The Yadkin is a river in North Carolina where I grew up."

Susan nodded but remained silent.

In an effort to draw her out, Rosalie said, "I haven't been on a horse's back since I fell off and ruined my shoulder. Have you ever fallen off a horse?"

"Have I! When I was eight I fell off and sprained my wrist. Then two years ago I fell off again and broke my leg real bad. That's why I walk funny."

"Weren't you afraid to ride again?"

Susan nodded vigorously. "After that first fall Papa made me get right on my horse again. I was back to riding before I even had a chance to think. The second time was a lot harder."

Rosalie was about to ask how the young girl had found the courage to ride again when they entered the stable and John drew their attention to a large tan mare with a red mane. "This here's Penny. She's a cross between a Clydesdale and a quarter horse. She's real steady in traffic." He moved to the next stall and pointed to a lighter tan gelding. "And this here's Nick—short for Nickel. He has Belgian and quarter horse in his blood. He's just a little bigger, but every bit as gentle."

Rosalie patted Nick's nose while Kenton entered the stall with John to give a closer inspection. The process was repeated with Penny, then Kenton focused on Rosalie.

"Which horse should we try?"

Rosalie shrugged.

Susan, who was stroking Penny's withers, told Kenton, "I think you should try Nick."

"Nick, it is. Will you ride with us, Miss Reddick?"

At a nod from her father she grinned broadly. "I'd be glad to."

Within minutes Judge had been taken into the stable and Nick hitched in his place. With Susan sitting on one side of him and Rosalie on the other, Kenton headed down the long drive and turned toward town. At a trot, Rosalie could easily tell that Nick's pace was more relaxed than that of a smaller horse, and in Traverse City traffic, the animal responded steady and sure to Kenton's commands. He asked her opinion as he neared the turn that would take them back toward Reddicks'.

She spoke confidently. "I think we should tell Mr. Reddick that Nick has passed his trial with flying colors." Without a pause, she changed topics. "Now that that's settled, I want Miss Reddick to tell me how she found the courage to ride horses again after she fell off and broke her leg."

"I couldn't have done it without Mr. McCune." Susan glanced at Kenton. The look on her face spoke of admiration, and something more. "It took a long time for my leg to mend. Mr. McCune would visit me and bring me my favorite candy."

Kenton smiled. "I've never known anyone so fond of chocolates as this young lady. I bought them for her from the Newtons before your aunt and uncle took over the confectionery."

Susan regarded Rosalie with new interest. "Your aunt and uncle own the Queen City Candy Shoppe?"

"They did until a few days ago. Someone else just took it over."

The young girl's face fell. "Their chocolates were the best. Better than Newtons. I had my fill of those the year I broke my leg, thanks to Mr. McCune!" She giggled.

Kenton turned to Susan. "But after your accident, there weren't enough chocolates in Michigan to entice you to get back on your horse."

"I should say not!"

Her curiosity growing, Rosalie asked, "So what changed your mind?"

Susan replied thoughtfully. "About the time Mr. McCune and Papa—and Mama, too—were trying to get me over my fear of riding, Mama started getting sickly. At first she just seemed tired and she'd sit down to rest a lot, but after awhile she couldn't keep up with her chores.

"Mama said maybe she just needed a visit with her own mother. But Grandma Ivy lives 'way over in Boston and Papa couldn't spare the time or money from the horse farm to take Mama there. Then one day Mr. McCune asked me if there was anything in this world that would get me to ride again. I told him if he could make my mama all better, I'd climb on a horse's back quicker than a scalded cat can jump out a back window."

Rosalie focused on Kenton. "Surely you didn't promise . . ."

Kenton shook his head. "I was in a real dilemma."

Susan continued. "Mr. McCune told me my mama's healing was in the Lord's hands but there was something he could do that might help. He said if I'd start riding again, he'd send me and Mama to Boston to visit Grandma Ivy."

Kenton took up the story. "The next time I visited Susan I pulled two round trip train tickets from my pocket and showed them to her."

Susan smiled. "I'll never forget that, because you tucked them away again as soon as I'd seen them. I thought you were an awful tease!"

"But my plan worked. You asked me to help you saddle up Penny." Kenton turned to Rosalie. "Penny is a gentler horse than the one Miss Reddick was riding when she fell. John had sold Susan's horse by then."

"My heart was beating pretty fast when Mr. McCune gave me a hand up," said Susan, "but by the time Penny had walked around the pasture I didn't feel so scared. The very next day Mr. McCune and Papa saw me and Mama off at the train station."

"Your mama looked better than she had in quite some time that day. Do you remember?"

Susan nodded. "But the farther we got from home, the weaker she got. I was afraid she wouldn't . . ." Susan lowered her gaze, her eyes welling up. Moisture prickled Rosalie's eyes as well.

Kenton continued. "Unfortunately, Susan's mother never saw Michigan again."

Rosalie said, "I'm so sorry, Miss Reddick."

Susan brushed away a tear and put on a sad smile. "It's okay. Mama lived to see Grandma, and that made her happy." After a moment's silence, she brightened. "So you see, Miss Foxe, I really didn't have enough courage all by myself to get on a horse again. If Mama hadn't taken sick, I might still be scared of them."

Rosalie pondered the thought. "But you succeeded in putting your fear aside, even if it was for the sake of your mother. You can be proud of yourself for that." Given similar circumstances, would Rosalie have been so courageous? She pushed the question aside as Kenton turned down the drive to the Reddick farm. "We're back and Nick is still performing admirably. It seems you've accomplished what you wanted, Mr. McCune. You've found a horse I can trust."

Kenton only smiled. He pulled to a stop and helped Rosalie down, then Susan. Mr. Reddick emerged from the stable to be quickly assured by Kenton that Nick had won approval.

Mr. Reddick issued a friendly warning. "Now McCune, don't wait so long to come visitin' again." To Rosalie, he said, "We've got plenty of trustworthy ridin' horses in all shades of brown. You're welcome to make use of them."

"Thanks for your kind offer, but I'll decline." To Kenton, she said, "We'd best be getting home. Mrs. Buckley will soon have dinner on."

CHAPTER 9

Later, when dinner had ended and Rosalie found herself in Kenton's company on the gazebo in the back yard, notions of horses fled from her mind and she recalled earlier thoughts about Cutler Gowen. She lowered the book she was holding but not reading, and dared to interrupt his concentration on the newspaper he held.

"Mr. McCune, I was thinking."

He folded the paper and focused on her, his half-smile inviting her to continue. For a moment all she could think about was the way the late afternoon sun enhanced the brown in his hazel and grey eyes, and the blond in his caramel-colored hair. Would she be thinking about these things when she went to work with him tomorrow morning?

He focused on her, as if studying the lace encircling her neck, and the loose strands of hair that were being teased by the wind. Then he reached for her book, lifting it enough to see the cover. When his hand brushed hers, a strange and disturbing sensation warmed her within, and she wanted both to pull away and to move closer. Doing neither, she struggled to remember what it was she had wanted to say, but he spoke instead.

"You're reading *Lord Jim*. What do you think of it?"

She forced herself to focus on the question. "I think Uncle Benjamin is right. It's Mr. Conrad's finest work." Remembering now her original question, she continued. "Mr. McCune, speaking of Uncle Benjamin, there are some things I don't understand at-all in regard to his store and the way he's being treated by Mr. Gowen."

Kenton's brows moved together. "Exactly what do you mean?"

"Not too long ago, he was acting mean enough to bite a snake. Then he comes over here Sunday leaking honey like an overflowing bee tree."

"He *is* a strange fellow—like Scrooge and Santa Clause all rolled into one."

"So why didn't he just make a decent offer to buy the place outright from the start? Instead, he got into a passel of problems with Miss Hackbardt and that plot of theirs to foreclose on the mortgage. Seems to me, he's spending a dollar to save a dime."

"Perhaps, but there's still plenty of money to be made in the candy business in Traverse City before Labor Day."

Rosalie sighed. "When I think of the way that Hackbardt woman lied to get Mr. Gowen his way, I could just paint her back porch red."

Growing pensive, Kenton continued. "The odd thing is that Mr. Gowen seems to believe Clarissa's story—that the payment was never made. Did you notice how consistent he's been? Every time the subject comes up he claims the double eagle you gave Miss Hackbardt for the July payment never existed."

Rosalie nodded. "Sunday was no exception. It put Uncle Benjamin and Mr. Gowen within a hog's hair of tussling."

"Maybe Miss Hackbardt and the missing coin aren't connected with Mr. Gowen in the way we assume."

Rosalie sighed. "I'd give anything to have a look in *all* of that woman's shoes."

Kenton remained thoughtful. When he spoke again, it was with an air of mystery. "Maybe the real reason for your aunt and uncle's problems lies in Mr. Gowen's past."

"Just what are you getting at, Mr. McCune?"

He leaned closer bringing with him the essence of sandalwood. "I have a feeling about the man. Something just isn't right. I've been making discreet inquiries, trying to find out where he came from and what he was doing before he built his candy factory."

She forced herself to ignore the pleasantly disturbing effects of Kenton's nearness and focus on the topic at hand. "And what have you learned about the infamous Cutler Gowen?"

"It's as if Mr. Gowen never existed until he showed up in Traverse City and announced plans to establish the American Candy Company. When you come to work with me tomorrow, you can help me track down his past—if there is one."

Rosalie nodded, fearing anew that come morning, her concentration on the history of Cutler Gowen would be difficult, at best, with the charming Kenton McCune so near at hand. She started to rise but he stopped her with a hand on her wrist.

"Before you go, there's something I'd like to ask you. I see from the paper that the circus is coming to town Saturday. Since circuses are for kids, and you and I are acquainted with a young lady who would enjoy the show, I was wondering if

perhaps the two of us should invite Susan as our guest?" He
opened the newspaper and pointed to an advertisement.

COMING!
TO TRAVERSE CITY
SATURDAY, AUGUST 4.

THE HIGHEST CLASS CIRCUS IN THE WORLD

THE GREAT WALLACE SHOWS

Three Rings, Half Mile Race Track, 1,000 Features
100 Phenomenal acts, 25 Clowns, 20 Hurricane Races
4 Trains. 1500 Employees, 6 Bands, 50 Cages
a Drove of Camels, 15 Open Dens, a Herd of Elephants.

$4000.00 DAILY EXPENSES.
The Purest, Cleanest, Mightiest, and Most Magnificent
Amusement Institution of the 19th Century.
The Greatest Performers in the known world are with the Great
Wallace Shows this season, including

THE NELSON FAMILY
Premier Acrobats of the World
THE ANGELOS – AERIALISTS
The 7 Stirks, Bicycle and Skating Experts
THE TEN DELLAMEADS-STATUARY ARTISTS MLLE.
NORDA FRENCH-MYSTERIOUS GLOBE
10 Principal Male and Female Equestrians
THE THREE PETITS, AERIAL BAR EXTRAORDINARY LEON
AND SINGING MULE "TRILBY"

The Sisters Vortex, Triple Revolving Trapeze
OUR STREET PARADE
At 10 am daily is the finest ever put on the streets. A sunburst of
splendor. A Triumph of Art, Money and Good Taste, with Lavish
Luxury of Spectacular Effect, and Greatest Professional Features
Conceivable.
**Excursions Run on Every Line of Travel. No Gambling Devices
Tolerated.**
NEVER DIVIDES. NEVER DISAPPOINTS.

Rosalie smiled as she returned Kenton's newspaper. "Mr.
McCune, I'd be delighted to go with you and Susan! I haven't
been to a circus since I was a very small child."

"Saturday it is, then! We'll make a day of it starting with
the parade at ten o'clock—if that's all right."

"By all means!"

~~~

But when Kenton drove Rosalie to Reddicks' the following
evening to invite Susan to the circus, he found John far less
receptive to the invitation than his daughter.

"A day at the circus is a day wasted," he grumbled, scuffing the gravel in the driveway as if impatient to get back to the
stable.

Susan lowered her gaze, her chin on her chest.

Kenton's heart wrenched. Why hadn't he mentioned this to
John in private first?

John stepped up to Susan, lifted her chin, and gazed loving-
ly into her eyes. "I suppose every kid ought to see the circus at

least once. If Mr. McCune and Miss Foxe want to take you, I suppose it's all right. Just remember, you still have Saturday chores to do."

She kissed his cheek impetuously. "Thanks, Papa. I won't forget!"

Kenton rested his hand on Susan's shoulder. "Would you do me a favor? Show Miss Foxe how well you ride around the ring while I talk to your father for a minute."

"Sure, Mr. McCune!" She turned to Rosalie, taking her by the hand. "Come with me, Miss Foxe!" The two walked off, Susan bubbling over with horse talk.

Alone with John, Kenton said, "Something's troubling you. Is there anything I can do to help?"

John kicked a small stone into the tall grass by the pasture fence post. "I'll make out." His gaze met Kenton's. "Didn't mean to come across like vinegar on a hot fudge sundae. Guess I'm more tired than I thought."

"Can't you hire someone to help out?"

Shifting toward the stable, John replied, "I had to let a man go today. Couldn't afford to keep him on. Now, unless there's somethin' else, I've got to get back to work."

Reluctant to leave, Kenton said, "There is one other thing, John." Knowing the man hadn't darkened the door of a church since his wife's funeral over a year ago, he cautiously suggested, "God will help, if you ask."

His friend's jaw grew taut, his cheeks suffusing with color. "I did all my askin' of God when Mary Claire took sick and we all know what come of that." He turned and strode toward the stable.

Later, as Kenton drove through the dusk toward home, Rosalie chattered with a description of what she'd seen in the riding ring, concluding, "That young Reddick girl certainly is a testimony to what a person can accomplish with a sufficient dose of determination."

Thank goodness, despite his discouraging conversation with John, his daughter had favorably impressed Rosalie just as he had hoped. Their conversation continued on other topics until Washington Street when Kenton brought it back to the Reddicks. Explaining that John was having business difficulties, he said, "I hope you won't think me out of place in asking, but would you please include Mr. Reddick in your prayers tonight? The Lord will know best how to supply his need."

As Kenton turned into his driveway, Rosalie replied, "I'll pray for him. And I'll ask Aunt Lottie and Uncle Benjamin to pray for him, too."

He brought the carriage to a halt by the side door and helped her down, continuing to hold her hand. "Thanks for coming with me tonight, and for your prayers."

Their gazes held and time stood still as the familiar essence of peach blossom filled Kenton's head, enticing him to kiss her temple, but as he bent closer, she backed away and broke contact.

"I'd best go and let the others know we're home." In a flash, she disappeared inside.

He stood staring at the door as it closed behind her, unable to suppress a smile. Surely, in a house full of open windows, she knew perfectly well that everyone had heard him drive in, and surely, she had debated with herself whether to let him kiss her. Perhaps next time . . .

CHAPTER 10

Kenton sat in the gazebo, reading the Saturday morning paper as he waited for Rosalie to get ready for the circus. A humorous story had him chuckling out loud as she came out the door and crossed the lawn to sit on the bench beside him.

"I'm pleased to see you've put the frustration of work behind you and are in good spirits this morning." She referred to the dead end they'd come up against in their investigation of Cutler Gowen during the previous two days at the law office.

He lowered the paper a tad. "Listen to this. 'A delightful watermelon party was enjoyed on the shore of the river in front of the residence of Frank Friedrich last evening. One of the watermelons had the misfortune to fall from the basket, and it rolled into the river and was drowned, but the other served the party most pleasantly. A jolly time was enjoyed by all.'"

Rosalie laughed outright. "That takes the whole biscuit! Until this minute, I didn't know a *watermelon* could drown."

Kenton folded the paper, his attention fully on her. The morning sun shimmered in her hair, setting a soft, amber frame about her oval face. He had an urge to take her off to some secluded spot along the bay for a private watermelon party of their own rather than Front Street which would be crowded with circus enthusiasts. He tried to banish the notion before it could take hold, remembering his commitment to Susan who was about to enjoy her very first circus, and the opportunity he would have in the evening to again be with Rosalie in greater privacy. Indicating the cloudless sky above, he struggled to redirect his thoughts to the plans for the morning, but his words sounded contemplative even to his own ears. "Looks like a fine day for a parade. We should go to Reddicks' and fetch our guest."

~~~

Rosalie caught the tentative tone in Kenton's voice—aware too, that she could easily forego a day at the circus with Susan for a day alone with Kenton. Despite the fact that she'd spent two long days with him at the office, they'd been too busy concentrating on routine legal tasks and the problem of Cutler Gowen for their personal friendship to flourish. They'd been too busy even to smile, and the way Kenton was looking at her now sent warmth through her that threatened to invade her cheeks. She lowered her gaze and drew a deep breath, then rose.

"Come along, Mr. McCune! We'd best get started for the Reddicks'. We've promised Susan a day she'll never forget."

Taking her by the elbow, he escorted her out of the gazebo. "Before we go, there's one thing I need from the house. Wait right here." A minute later he reappeared wearing a red stovepipe hat with a tall white ostrich plume tucked into its wide blue and white striped hat band.

Rosalie eyed him skeptically. "I can't exactly say you're the height of fashion, but you're patriotic."

"I'm sure I look more like a clown than like Uncle Sam, but this *is* a day for clowns. At least you and Susan will always know where I am."

Kenton drove the back streets out of town to avoid the main routes congested with circus traffic. The moment Susan saw Kenton she teased him mercilessly about his hat, then insisted he let her try it on. When it fell down covering her entire face, Rosalie laughed till her sides were sore. Then she tried it on herself, angling it in different directions while Kenton and Susan took their turns laughing.

Placing his novel top hat on his head again, Kenton drove back to town and parked his carriage at home, away from the crowds in the heart of the city. He escorted Rosalie and Susan the few short blocks to the west end of Front Street where hundreds of people were already starting to congregate. Susan's excitement began to infect Rosalie as the young girl chatted.

"I can hardly wait to see the equestrians! Papa says they ride around the ring standing on the horses' backs, and leap from one horse to another. He says some can even do a backward somersault and land on a different horse!"

Rosalie was about to confirm Susan's expectations when the young girl stopped dead and pointed to the opposite side of the street. "Look at the candy shop!"

Rosalie hadn't been past the store her aunt and uncle had owned since Thursday afternoon when Kenton had driven Nick down Front Street. The prominent white sign she now saw above the door literally made her choke. Kenton read it out loud.

"'Clarissa's Confections.'" The bold crimson proclamation was accompanied by slightly smaller blue lettering beneath. "'American Candy Company.' If that doesn't take all!"

Regaining control of herself, Rosalie asked indignantly, "Do you believe it, Mr. McCune? *Clarissa's* Confections?"

Susan asked innocently, "Who's Clarissa?"

Kenton answered, "A troublesome acquaintance of ours."

"I can't believe she's actually tending shop herself," said Rosalie.

Starting across the street, Kenton said, "I can't either, but I'm going to find out if she is."

Rosalie held back. "You don't really intend to patronize the place, do you?"

With a mischievous smile, he said, "It's time I treat Susan to some chocolates. No telling what that simple act might reveal."

Crossing the street with Kenton and Susan, Rosalie paused on the walk a few yards away from the confectionery. At least a dozen children were crowded around its front window. Though curious as to the reason, Rosalie remained determined to keep her distance. "You two go on in. I can't bring myself to step foot in a place with Miss Hackbardt's name on it after what she's already put Aunt Lottie and Uncle Benjamin through."

The bell on the screen door of the candy shop jingled constantly as Rosalie waited for Kenton and Susan to return. Rumors of an accident on the road and a delay of the parade floated around her as more people gathered along the street. A few minutes later Susan and Kenton were again at her side, the young girl licking an elephant-shaped red lollipop.

Susan paused in her indulgence to say, "They didn't have any chocolates, or any fudge, but the lady in there gave me this!"

Kenton explained further. "Miss Hackbardt was very much in evidence—not working, mind you, but acting as a sort of greeter and handing out samples. She said the dipped chocolates and fudge will be available again after your aunt and uncle come to work at Mr. Gowen's factory next week."

"You ought to see the circus display in their window, Miss Foxe," said Susan. "There are hard candies in every shape and color showing the different acts. The center ring even has elephants that move in a circle, all linked together, trunk to tail!"

"No wonder so many children are pressed against the window," Rosalie concluded.

Kenton pulled a wrapped butterscotch from his pocket and offered it to her. "Miss Hackbardt inquired about you. When I told her you were right outside, she insisted I give you this."

Despite her aversion to the giver, Rosalie was tempted to accept the candy, remembering the delicious sample Mr. Gowen had provided the night of the carnival ball, but she put her hand up. "You keep it."

Susan pulled her lollipop from her mouth long enough to ask Kenton, "What time is it? I thought the parade would have started by now."

Just then, the sheriff came riding down the center of the street making an announcement through a megaphone. "Please be patient! The circus parade will begin in thirty minutes!"

Rosalie expected a grumble from Susan, but the girl only shrugged. "I'm glad I've got this lollipop to pass the time, if we're going to have to wait."

Catching sight of Cutler Gowen approaching, Rosalie nudged Kenton. "It appears the boss has come to check on his new business."

When Cutler Gowen had disappeared inside the confectionery, Kenton said, "If you ladies will excuse me, I have a sudden need for some hard candies."

When he had gone, Rosalie turned to Susan. "I guess that leaves the two of us to keep up conversation."

Susan took her lollipop from her mouth. "I already told you most of my story, so I'd just as soon you did the talking. Besides, I never knew anyone from North Carolina. What's it like there?"

Rosalie described Old North State in generalities from the Atlantic Coast in the east to the Piedmont in the central section, to the Blue Ridge Mountains beyond.

Then Susan asked about Rosalie's family and schooling. The young girl listened with rapt attention, learning of the traditions at Tanglewood, and at Salem Academy—the birthday celebration of the president of the school each September, the candlelight service and love feast held on Christmas Eve in Old Home Church, and the celebration of Christ during Easter week with another love feast. Rosalie had begun a description of summers in the mountain resort of Blowing Rock when the sound of band music in the distance caught her attention.

"I believe the circus parade is coming!"

Susan tipped her ear, then cast a backward glance at the confectionery. "Mr. McCune had better come soon, or he'll miss the start of it!"

On cue the appearance of a red top hat—easily visible above the crowd—marked his emergence from the candy store. Cutler Gowen and Clarissa followed behind, blending into the crowd several feet to the left of Rosalie and Susan.

When Kenton took his place beside Rosalie, she said, "Mr. Gowen must have been quite talkative."

Kenton nodded. "He had plenty to say all right. And almost every word concerned the candy business."

"Did you ask him what he was doing before he came to Traverse City?"

Kenton nodded. "He said he traveled a lot, then he went right back to the subject of candy and what a fine job Clarissa has been doing."

With the strains of *Yankee Doodle* growing louder, Rosalie gave up on conversation and focused on the parade coming into view. A huge bandwagon led the way, drawn by a team of six plumed white horses arrayed in silver-studded tack. The wagon itself, painted white with golden swans carved in high relief, was identified with the Wallace name arcing above the birds.

The band was followed closely by a float carrying a lovely tableau of young ladies clad in filmy white dresses and ballet slippers, their slim, elegant forms supported by the shoulders of strong young men in tunics and leotards. Behind them, a long flatbed wagon offered three pairs of acrobatic performers enough space to demonstrate a sampling of their gymnastic skills. The cartwheels and handsprings of the men reminded Rosalie of Bobby Dan, the younger brother of her good friend, Willy Jo. The mid-air somersaults of both the men and the young ladies who landed in their arms made Rosalie gasp. How did they manage such stunts on a moving wagon?

Next came a contingent of clowns weaving a humorous path from one side of the street to the other, colliding and falling down, then picking each other up so forcefully they would fall again. One clown carried a bouquet of balloons. He offered one to Susan, then quick as a wink, stole Kenton's hat! Making an effort to place it on his orange mop-like hair, he pranced around causing gales of laughter, teased Clarissa by temporarily setting it on her head, then returned it to Kenton's head with a bow.

Behind the clowns came three squads of spirited ponies in gilt bridles and reins, their equestrian performers riding bareback. Susan pointed to the smallest pony carrying the smallest rider—a little girl wearing leotard, tights, slippers, and a puffy little pink skirt.

"She can't be more than five years old, and look how well she rides!"

Kenton nodded and smiled. "She'll probably steal the show when the equestrian act takes the ring."

The little girl atop the pony was followed by animals in cages on wheels. A lion with a huge mane announced his presence with a roar. Tigers, leopards, and a gorilla followed in line. The next wagon, divided across the center, held three chimpanzees in the front half and several smaller monkeys in the rear. The chimps swung from their swings and the bars of their cage, squealing and laughing with raucous delight while the smaller monkeys hung by their tails or flitted about their quarters with ease and grace. The animals had just gone by when shouts rose from onlookers to the right. Susan darted into the street to see what was happening before Rosalie or Kenton could stop her.

"The monkeys are loose!" she cried.

Someone else said, "The chimpanzees are out, too!"

Confusion reigned as the parade came to a halt. Suddenly, monkeys and chimpanzees seemed to be everywhere. One monkey leaped from person to person across shoulders stealing hats at will and tossing them aside. When he came to Ken-Kenton, he swiped the tall red hat and ran off down the street.

Susan jammed the stick of her lollipop into Rosalie's hand. "I'm going after him!"

She took off before either Rosalie or Kenton could protest.

"I'll fetch her," said Kenton.

Behind Rosalie, someone said, "Look! The monkeys have gotten into the candy shop!"

She turned to find Clarissa trying unsuccessfully to chase monkeys and chimpanzees away from the front of the store with a broom while Cutler Gowen and one of his lady clerks tossed an unwanted invader—his fists full of licorice—out the front door.

A moment later the monkey carrying Kenton's hat reappeared, leaping from the sign on the neighboring store to the awning of the candy shop. He paused there to swing back and forth. When Kenton and Susan caught up with him, he taunted them with a hideous laugh.

Susan shook her finger at him. "You naughty boy! Come down this instant!"

Kenton reached slowly for the monkey. "Nice fellow. Now come to me."

Rosalie offered Susan's lollipop to the monkey as an enticement. "Here, boy, come on down and get a treat."

Clarissa pushed in front of them, claiming, "I can get that rascal down." She raised her broom and swung it at the monkey.

The hat went flying.

The monkey fell into Kenton's arms.

When the rascal tried to scramble away, Kenton gripped him tightly by the wrists, claiming, "Your tricks are up, little fellow!"

Just then, Cutler Gowen opened the door to evict two chimps. Seeing an opportunity, the monkey Kenton was holding bit him on the hand to free himself, retrieved Kenton's hat from the walk, and scrambled inside.

Kenton rubbed the back of his hand. "That little scamp!"

Rosalie turned on Clarissa. "Now look what you've done!"

Clarissa dropped her broom to inspect Kenton's hand. "I'm sorry! I didn't mean for that to happen."

Rosalie wanted to pick up the broom and swat Clarissa's behind. The thought evaporated when a chimpanzee ran out of the store carrying Kenton's hat filled to the brim with candy.

Cutler Gowen followed in hot pursuit. "Catch that chimp!"

When Kenton and Susan took up the chase, Rosalie hurried after them, but the crowd was so thick she soon lost sight of the hat, the chimp, and both of her friends. All of Front Street was mayhem, the parade stalled in its tracks while every member of the circus and all those who had come to watch the parade set about returning the monkeys and chimps to their cage. Rosalie was working her way back to the confectionery to wait for Susan and Kenton when the young girl caught up with her, Kenton's hat in hand.

"Look what I found, Miss Foxe!" Susan beamed. "It's not very clean and half of the candy is missing, but at least I got it back."

Several hard candies and small lollipops remained in the hat—and the glimmer of something more. She reached in to pull out a chased gold money clip fat with bills. Flipping through them, she began to count the cash, but gave up when she lost count, realizing that most of the currency was in large denominations.

Shoving the money clip into her skirt pocket, she told Susan, "Mr. McCune will know what to do with it." Scouring the crowd for Kenton, she spotted him some yards away, headed toward her.

Moments later the young girl presented him with his half-full hat. "It's soiled, but it's not dented."

"Good job, Miss Reddick." Kenton glanced at the candy, then handed the hat back to Susan. "You'd better return the sweets to the confectionery."

When the young girl had departed, Rosalie said, "Come with me, Mr. McCune, there's something I want to show you." Away from the hub of the crowd, she gave Kenton the money clip. "This was inside your hat when Susan found it. I don't know how much is there."

Kenton whistled softly as he counted the money, pausing to study some of the bills as if determining their authenticity. His brow twitched at the discovery of a newspaper clipping buried in the center of the stack of currency. He tucked the money in his pants pocket and began to read the article to Rosalie.

"'Lazarus Ambrose Dead. New York Central Conductor Killed by Ruffians. Lazarus Ambrose, a twenty-year employee of the New York Central Railroad, was found dead this morning in an alley near his Cherry Street home, the apparent victim of assault and robbery. The suspects are still at large. The bachelor leaves one brother, two sisters, and several nieces and nephews in the city. Due to the brutal nature of his demise, a closed casket funeral will be held at the home of his sister, Mrs. William Spicer, Saturday at one o'clock, directed by W.S. Vincent. Mr. Ambrose was forty years old." Focusing on Rosalie, Kenton wondered, "Why would this be kept in a money clip?"

She shrugged. "Mr. Ambrose must have been a friend of the man who lost this money."

"A friend, or a victim?" Kenton asked as he refolded the article and tucked it into the gold clip where he'd found it.

Chills ran down Rosalie's spine. "That's a frightening prospect, Mr. McCune—that the man who lost this money might be a ..."

"Murderer?" He slipped the cash back into his pants pocket. "I'm going to turn the entire problem over to Sheriff Rennie just as soon as I can find him."

Seconds after he'd spoken those words, Cutler Gowen appeared with Susan. "Miss Reddick says you found a money clip in your hat. It's mine, and I can identify it."

Kenton regarded him skeptically. "I'm listening, Mr. Gowen."

Rosalie reached for Susan's hand, drawing her away from Gowen while listening intently to his every word.

"If the monkeys didn't lose any of my money while they were on their rampage, there are ..." he paused. Drawing Kenton near, he spoke in confidential tones.

Kenton stood back. "Your description is correct, as far as it goes."

Gowen thought a moment, his expression transforming from troubled to melancholy. "There was one other item in my clip, a notice of the death of ..." he paused to swallow, his eyes growing misty. When he spoke again, it was with reverence and respect. " ... my lifelong friend, Lazarus Ambrose. I loved him like a brother, may he rest in peace."

Kenton handed over the money clip.

Mr. Gowen started to put it away, then evidently thinking better of it, pealed off two bills and offered them to Kenton. "Your reward for finding and returning my money."

Kenton shook his head. "If anyone deserves a reward, Miss Reddick does."

Gowen stepped up to the young girl and stuffed the bills into her hand. "Don't spend it all in one place—unless, of course, you decide to patronize Clarissa's Candy!"

Susan stared at the pair of one hundred dollar bills in awe. "Thank you, Mr. Gowen! Thank you!"

As Gowen walked away, the last contingent of the circus parade was announced by clowns who proceeded down either side of Front Street, shouting "Hold your horses! The elephants are coming!" In the distance, the calliope could be heard.

Susan turned to Kenton, her face the definition of delight. "So much has happened already, I almost forgot! We haven't even been to the circus, yet!" Shoving her money into his hand, she asked, "Will you please keep this for me until I get home?" Not waiting for an answer, she hurried to the edge of the walk.

Kenton hadn't even had time to tuck her money into his own clip when she turned to beckon. "Mr. McCune, Miss Foxe, come look!"

As Rosalie and Kenton took places on either side of the Susan, a smile beamed across her young face. A drove of elephants—huge mama and papa bulls followed tail to trunk by their baby offspring in fancy oriental coats—lumbered down the street.

Behind them, the street cleaners shoveled elephant-sized droppings into wheelbarrows while the calliope brought up the rear of the parade with a lively rendition of *Where Did You Get That Hat?*

When the rolling steam organ had passed by, Kenton offered an arm to each of his lady friends. "We'd best follow the music to the circus grounds. There are bound to be some interesting side shows to watch before the start of the performances in the rings."

CHAPTER 11

"How can he swallow fire?" Susan asked Kenton as one of the Alphonzos inserted a flaming stick into his mouth at the circus side show.

He shrugged. "I've always wondered that myself. Miss Foxe, do you know?"

"I'm afraid I don't know anything at-all about fire eaters. But even if I did, I wouldn't tell. It would spoil your fun!"

A larger flame disappeared down the throat of the performer garnering Susan's enthusiastic applause. "This is the best show I've ever seen!"

Kenton chuckled, pleased that his young charge was enjoying a break from the daily chores and training at her father's stables. "This is only the side show. Wait until you see the performers in the rings!"

When the ventriloquist, contortionists, puppeteers, snake charmer, strong man, knife and hatchet throwers, and minstrels had completed their acts, Kenton escorted Rosalie and Susan to front row seats by the center ring.

Having purchased a candy apple for Susan, a bag of popcorn for Rosalie, and some peanuts for himself, Kenton settled down beside his lady guests to watch in awe as the lion trainer entered the cage with several lions, a small buggy whip in hand. With precise cracks, the trainer signaled his animals on-to stools, through hoops, and over one another leap-frog style. Then he set a ring on fire. All the cats jumped through on command except one. The last lion, the largest of all, pawed at the trainer, knocked his whip from his hand, then gave chase. The trainer ran from the cage, slammed the door shut just in time to prevent the lion's escape, then returned to successfully coax the lion through the hoop before dousing the fire.

Susan clapped furiously.

Kenton exchanged glances with Rosalie who was smiling at the young girl's reaction, just as he was. Silently, he gave thanks for a day which, despite early setbacks, was turning into real fun for the Reddick girl and a pleasant outing for Rosalie as well. He was thankful, too, that new light had been shed on the mystery surrounding Gowen.

His private thoughts ended when Susan pointed to the ring to their left.

"Look! The equestrians! I've been waiting all day for this!"

A white Lippizaner pranced into the ring and began circling it. The little girl who had ridden in the parade, now ran into the ring, paused to curtsy, then ran to a launching platform and sprang to a standing position on the horse's bare hind quarters. Susan turned to Kenton and Rosalie, her face a puzzle.

"How does she stay on?"

"With resin," said Rosalie. "Equestrians put lots of resin on their slippers and on their horses' backs. They have a special name for their horses, too. Resinbacks!"

"You know a lot about circus horses," said Kenton.

"Gaspar told me about them." To Susan, she said, "Gaspar is the hired man who traveled with the circus before he came to work for my Daddy."

Susan nodded, her attention again riveted by new horses and performers entering the ring. A woman dressed in white satin created a lovely tableau with the little girl, posing on the points of her ballet slippers. Their stunts were enhanced by the addition of a white dog jumping on and off the horse's back, and white doves which perched on their shoulders.

Their feminine expertise was followed by a young man with a vaulting act. Running alongside his horse, he held a handgrip that was attached to the harness. Executing somer-saults and cartwheels, he then sprang onto the horse in a back-facing position and scissored around to the front.

When the gymnast exited the ring, an older man entered, standing astride two white horses. Rosalie told Susan, "That's called *La Poste,* after the French word for courier. Watch what comes next."

Another horse entered the ring following closely behind the first two. They split apart and the third horse passed between the rider's legs while he picked up its reins. The process was repeated again and again until the rider was in control of an eight-horse team. They exited the ring to thunderous applause.

Susan turned to Kenton, her face bright with enthusiasm. "That's the most exciting horse riding I've ever seen in my life! I wish Papa could have come. He'd have loved it!"

Kenton smiled. "Maybe next time *he'll* bring you."

She shook her head. "All he ever wants to do is work."

As a bear act filed into the ring to the far right, Susan told Kenton and Rosalie, "I don't think the rest of the circus could be as good as the horses."

But she applauded just as loudly for the bears that balanced on balls and tight ropes; the Dellameades who posed in scenes of history and mythology; the Stirk family who performed hand stands and other feats on moving bicycles; the tramp bicyclist, Edie Penaud; the Japanese jugglers who kept five pins in the air simultaneously; the trapeze artists who somersaulted backward to be caught in mid-air; and the high wire walkers who leaped over one another.

And there was no indication that the final act, the elephants, was any less extraordinary or amazing to Susan than its predecessors. She appeared utterly fascinated by the mammoth animals who could stand on their front legs or their back legs, turn pirouettes on tubs, push one of their offspring around the ring in an oversized buggy, and ride bicycles.

When an elephant held a beautiful woman in his mouth and spun around, Susan told Kenton and Rosalie, "The elephants are just as good as the equestrians!"

Rosalie said, "And they're not finished yet. Watch closely."

While one elephant stood stationary, another elephant placed front feet on his hind quarters. One, by one, other elephants stacked up in a row until ten huge animals formed an impressive line.

Applauding with gusto, Susan said, "I was wrong. The elephants are even *better* than the horses!"

Kenton grinned. "That's quite an admission, coming from you!"

As the band played a rousing exit piece, Kenton escorted Rosalie and Susan out of the tent. The young miss was full of chatter all the way to Washington Street. He was thankful that she kept Rosalie entertained on the gazebo while he managed a secret conference with the Marshalls and Mrs. Buckley, hitched Nick to his buggy, then returned to the house to collect a chipboard box which he stowed in the compartment at the rear of the carriage.

Susan's enthusiasm for the circus didn't wane even on the drive home. When Kenton helped her out of his buggy, she was in such a rush to tell her father about her day that she hurried off without her reward money.

Kenton called after her. "Miss Reddick, aren't you forgetting something?" He took the bills from his pocket and held them in the breeze.

At the same time, her father emerged from the stable. When the two of them arrived at the carriage, Susan was still bubbling over with descriptions of her day. ". . . and you should have seen the elephants and the horses!"

Mr. Reddick smiled, but his face and his voice held the same weariness as before.

"You had a good day, I take it."

"Oh, yes! And I've got to tell you what happened at the parade! The monkeys—"

Her father cut her off. "Enough for now, Susan. Go change and do your chores. Day's almost done."

Her face fell, her exuberance replaced by resignation as she slowly turned away.

Rosalie stepped out of the buggy. "Miss Reddick, wait!" To John, she said, "Begging your indulgence, sir, but your daughter and Mr. McCune have some news that's guaranteed to make you feel more terrific than a turkey in young corn."

Kenton held Susan's reward money in front of John. "Your daughter earned cash money today. Two hundred dollars." He handed the bills to his friend.

John gave them a good looking over as if suspicious of their authenticity. Seemingly convinced they were genuine, he focused on Susan. "Money like this don't grow on trees any more than horses do. Where'd you get it?"

Evidently unsure where to begin, Susan turned to Kenton. "You tell him, Mr. McCune!" Not waiting for his explanation, she hurried toward the house.

Rosalie went after her.

Alone with John, Kenton briefly told about the escaped monkeys and his stolen hat. "Mr. Gowen, the owner of the new candy factory in town, lost his money clip, and Susan found it in my hat along with some candy. This is her reward."

A silent moment lapsed—a long moment in which John's skeptical look melted into one of gratification. His eyes clouded over as he folded the bills and pressed them into his breeches pocket. "Thank you, Mr. McCune. You know I was in bad need of this."

"Don't thank me. Thank God," Kenton advised reverently. "This money is answered prayer."

John's fair cheeks began to flush. "Answered prayer? It was a passel of monkey business, if you ask me."

"God used monkeys to answer prayers."

"I didn't do any prayin'," John asserted.

Kenton grinned. "No, but I did, and so did Miss Foxe and her aunt and uncle."

John's color deepened. "You didn't—"

"No point in working yourself into a stew, John. None of them knew you were short of money, they only knew you needed help with your business, and that the Lord would know best how to supply it."

John rubbed his boot in the dirt, evidently contemplating the thought. His cool blue eyes meeting Kenton's, he said, "I think it was coincidence. But I'm thankful to you for takin' Susan to the circus." Taking the bills from his pocket to look at them again, he chuckled softly. "Just thinkin' that two days back I was convinced that circus was nothin' but a waste of time."

Kenton wanted to press his point about answered prayer, but decided against it when he saw that Rosalie was about to join them.

Addressing John, she said, "Do you remember telling me the other day that you have plenty of riding horses in brown?"

He nodded. "You're welcome to make use of 'em anytime you want. Got a real gentle chestnut mare that'd be just right for a lady such as yourself. Want to see her?"

Color rose in her cheeks. "I . . . uh . . . maybe another time. It's getting late." To Kenton, she said, "Mrs. Buckley will be angry if we're late for supper."

On the drive to town, it was all Kenton could do to keep from bringing up the subject of riding. Rosalie remained quiet, and he suspected she was contemplating the prospect still. His suspicions were confirmed when she finally broke the silence several minutes later.

"I've been thinking, Mr. McCune, and I've come to a profound conclusion."

A long pause ensued during which Kenton held his breath and prayed that Rosalie would overcome her estrangement from horses. He was about to prompt her when she continued.

"I've come to the conclusion that courage can't be borrowed. It can be contagious for a time, in a superficial sort of way, but real courage definitely cannot be borrowed."

"Then you agree somewhat with a man named Prentice. He once said, 'Courage, like cowardice, is undoubtedly contagious, but some persons are not liable to catch it.' I think your perception is much deeper and wiser." Kenton continued to ponder the thought, adding, "I have a belief about the true source of courage."

When a silent moment had lapsed, Rosalie said, "I'm waiting for you to enlighten me! Goodness knows my understanding is less than complete."

"And so is mine," Kenton warned her, "but there is One who has all the answers. One who's the source of courage if we ask, and His help is never superficial."

Following a silent moment, Rosalie said, "I suppose you are right to say that God is the source of courage, but in order to access it, you have to ask Him. A person could be too frightened to even ask help to get over what scares him or her."

"Then I suppose that would call for some extra special prayer." Though Kenton was tempted to launch into a speech on the advantages of overcoming fears and personal demons, he forced himself to lay the topic aside and focus on his driving.

~~~

Rather than turning right on the route toward Washington Street, Kenton kept Nick on a straight path toward the bay and the docks, setting Rosalie on edge.

"I assume you have a purpose for taking a longer way home, Mr. McCune. I hate to think we'll be any later than necessary for Mrs. Buckley's dinner. She can dish out quite a serving of wrath when occasion warrants."

He turned to her with a grin. "Miss Foxe, I have a confession to make. We're not eating supper at home tonight."

"But what about—"

"It's all arranged with Mrs. Buckley. I apologize for not saying so when we were at the Reddicks', but I didn't want to mention then that I've planned a surprise for you tonight—an evening cruise and concert on the bay and a box supper on the grounds of the Ne-ah-ta-wanta Resort. I hope you're not too tired to enjoy it."

"Too tired? Of course not! It sounds like a perfectly lovely way to finish our day." As he parked near the end of a long, wide pier and retrieved their box lunch from the storage compartment, her thoughts drifted back to that morning on the gazebo. She'd had fleeting thoughts of a day alone with Kenton, but his plans for this evening were far nicer.

He escorted her onto a dock she'd visited several times on her missions to scare up candy customers. On the left was a huge lake steamer, the *Illinois,* taking on overnight passengers and cargo for distant ports. She'd stood in awe of it many times before, and tonight's close-up view of its dark hull and stack, rows of lifeboats perched on the top deck, and line of cabins beneath was no less fascinating.

Opposite the *Illinois* on the right side of the pier floated the Traverse Bay Line's smaller boat, *Columbia,* ready for excursion passengers to come aboard. In the center of the dock between the two vessels stood the little square building where tickets were sold, a sign above its door reading, *Crescent Band Moonlight Cruise Tonight—6:30.* Kenton had soon purchased two twenty-five cent tickets and ushered her onto the upper deck of the boat, choosing seats inside the lounge a comfortable distance from the band and affording a good view of the scenery.

But Rosalie couldn't stay seated for long. Once underway she roamed the deck, studying the landmarks on shore. Kenton identified them for her as they grew smaller—the Wequetong Clubhouse just east of the Boardman River; the three stacks of the Oval Wood Dish Company and the single stack of the Beitner Company, all on distant Boardman Lake; and the Greilick Sawmill at the foot of Division Street.

In the opposite direction, a small island in the center of the bay came slowly into view, its wooded shores transforming from a gray-green haze in the distance to a deeper forest green as the *Columbia* steamed past. A few minutes later a point of land drew Rosalie's attention, and the Ne-ah-ta-wanta Resort distinguished by white siding, dark roofed gables and a multi-windowed center tower came clearly into view.

Once onshore, Kenton led her to an umbrella table with a perfect view of the bay, the island, and the setting sun. Placing the box lunch in front of her, he said, "Why don't you start unpacking supper while I fetch us suitable beverages."

While Rosalie set out the roast beef sandwiches, celery and carrot sticks, fresh peaches, and jam-filled sugar cookies Mrs. Buckley had packed, she noticed that other passengers had chosen to spend their time strolling the beautifully manicured lawn or partaking in games of croquet and badminton. The happy voices of children at play in a distant side yard blended delightfully with the evening songs of the robins and sparrows flitting from tree to bush, and the calls of gulls over the water. She watched them soar low, then dive into the water for their dinner, thinking how different was Grand Traverse Bay from her home in the Piedmont of North Carolina. Her thoughts had drifted from North Carolina, to the circus, to the strange happenings with Cutler Gowen when Kenton returned with two glasses of root beer.

He sat beside her and asked a blessing on their meal, then reached for a carrot stick, chewing contemplatively until sharing his thoughts. "We learned some things about Mr. Gowen today."

Rosalie set aside her roast beef sandwich. "I was thinking that very thing when you were fetching the root beer."

"He had a lifelong friend by the name of Lazarus Ambrose."

"An Ambrose who lived on Cherry Street and was a conductor for the New York Central."

Kenton nodded. "Now if we only knew what city. I'm willing to guess that just about every town connected to the New York Central has a Cherry Street."

"But only one has a Mrs. Spicer who would have been Ambrose's sister. I could write letters of inquiry on Monday," Rosalie offered.

Kenton jabbed the air with a celery stick. "Or better yet, send telegrams."

Rosalie pondered the suggestion. "Mr. McCune, I hope you won't take me wrong in what I'm about to say, but I still think Clarissa Hackbardt was mainly at fault for Aunt Lottie and Uncle Benjamin's troubles. Now that Mr. Gowen has been willing to make amends, is it really so important to delve into his past?"

"No man covers his tracks as well as Gowen has unless he's got something very important to hide. We spent all of Thursday and Friday checking with Mr. Johnson at the bank and Miss Welsh at the Western Union Office, and what did we find?"

Rosalie sighed, recalling the futility of their efforts. "No out-of-town bank drafts, no telegrams sent or received aside from those pertinent to the building and running of his candy factory."

"Exactly. Something's amiss and I won't be satisfied until I find out what it is."

Rosalie nibbled on her sandwich. Despite Kenton's concentration on Gowen, she was still pondering the conundrum of Clarissa. "I'm curious as to how Miss Hackbardt linked up with your nemesis. Did they know each other before Mr. Gowen came to town?"

"No, they didn't, and please believe me when I say you don't want to know the occasion of their meeting." Delving into his sandwich with gusto, he paused between bites to push a cookie in her direction. "If you don't like your sandwich, at least eat a cookie."

A sick feeling settled in the pit of her stomach. She pushed the cookie away, watching him finish his sandwich and begin on his own cookie. "You must have somehow fostered Gowen's and Clarissa's association."

He polished off the last bite of his cookie and smiled. "Miss Foxe, do you realize you are wasting a perfectly lovely Saturday evening at the Ne-ah-ta-wanta Resort talking about unpleasant business that will only lead to indigestion?"

"You brought it up—the talk about business, I mean."

He raised his hands palm out. "Guilty as charged! Now let's put it aside until Monday and concentrate on a subject more pleasant and sweet, such as Mrs. Buckley's raspberry jam-filled sugar cookies. You really should try yours." He slid it in front of her again.

Though tempted to argue, the contrite look on his face, now being drawn into an exaggerated, pleading expression, made her chuckle.

Reaching for the cookie, she said, "Business aside until Monday."

CHAPTER 12

On Monday, Rosalie learned that Kenton had indeed brought Clarissa Hackbardt and Cutler Gowen together. But her anger took flight when she read a telegram informing her that her mother and sister would be arriving from North Carolina midweek for a month-long visit.

When Wednesday arrived, and her mother and sister had been welcomed warmly by Kenton, Aunt Lottie, and Uncle Ben, Rosalie helped Vanda Mae unpack in her bedroom. Her entire focus now was on news from home. On the ride from the train depot, she'd learned how her sister's favorite horse had been stolen on Friday night when Willy Jo had ridden it to Salem, and how she'd hurt her shoulder the following afternoon, thus causing her father's hasty plans to send her mother and sister to Traverse City. Now, Rosalie pried for other news.

"Aside from Daddy being terribly disappointed about your horse and your accident, how is he?"

Vanda Mae paused as she placed her underthings in the drawer Rosalie had cleared for her. "Daddy's fine—at least as far as his health is concerned, but he's been cross as a bear with two cubs and a sore toe since he heard the news Gaspar gave him Sunday morning."

Having hung one of her sister's dresses in the closet, Rosalie turned with curiosity to Vanda Mae. "The only way Gaspar could displease Daddy is if there's something wrong with his driving horses. Did one of them take sick?"

Vanda Mae flicked her long, dark hair off her shoulder. "Worse. They were both missing from the south pasture that morning. There weren't any holes in the fence, either. They just vanished without a trace!"

A few quiet moments lapsed while Rosalie rearranged hat boxes on her closet shelf to make room for Vanda Mae's. Her sister tried to help, but in her injured state, her assistance caused more problems than it solved.

Laughing at her own ineptitude, Vanda Mae said, "I'm just going to get out of your way and let you arrange things. You're far more practiced using your left hand than I shall ever be." She had started to back out of the closet when she paused to inspect a pair of ladies' knickerbockers hanging on the rod. "I've never known you to own a pair of these. Have you taken up cycling since you came north?"

Rosalie's face grew warm. "No. I ... uh ... Mr. McCune bought those for me thinking it would help me gather the courage to ..."

"To ride tandem with him? What a romantic notion, touring the city on a bicycle built for two. Of course, balancing will be—"

"The knickerbockers aren't intended for the purpose of cycling," Rosalie said, trying to shoo Vanda Mae out of her way.

The young girl remained planted, hand on hip. "What then?"

Rosalie's cheeks burned. "If you must know, I'm considering getting on a horse again."

"Rosalie!" Vanda Mae gasped with obvious delight.

"Mr. McCune wanted to buy me a fancy, expensive riding habit but I told him that might be a complete waste, if I never actually put my foot into a stirrup."

Leading Rosalie away from the closet to a straight-backed chair, Vanda Mae pulled up another one for herself. "Sit down this minute and tell me how Mr. McCune managed to revive your interest in horseback riding."

Rosalie did as she was asked, sharing the story of Susan Reddick, finishing with, "I know you'd like her. Perhaps Mr. McCune will take us all to the Reddick place soon, so you two can meet."

Vanda Mae scowled.

"Now, you've got a face like a mule eating briars," Rosalie gently scolded.

With a sigh, Vanda Mae explained. "As punishment for riding the Steadmans' racing horse when I promised not to, Daddy has forbidden me to get on a horse again for a month." Suddenly brightening, she added, "But I want to meet Susan and her daddy and see their horses, and I surely want to be there when you ride again."

"Don't get your heart set on my doing it anytime soon. I'm about a ton short on courage."

Vanda Mae winked mischievously. "Then I'm going to start praying for that ton to be delivered post haste."

Rosalie reached for Vanda Mae's hand, giving it a squeeze, then took up conversation on a new topic. "Tell me, how is Bobby Dan?" When Vanda Mae rolled her eyes, Rosalie quickly amended her question. "You know what I mean, other than the usual handsprings, cartwheels, and crazy antics he's always pulling."

Unsmiling, Vanda Mae replied, "He pulled the biggest antic of them all three days ago."

"I hope he didn't hurt himself doing acrobatics."

Moving to the fainting couch, Vanda Mae leaned back. "I'll tell you what happened."

Rosalie listened intently as her sister relayed Willy Jo's description of the spat concerning himself, Bobby Dan, and his father.

Vanda Mae continued. "So Bobby Dan up and ran away from home the very next night, and nobody knows where he's gone. Of course, Mrs. Winthrop is beside herself, and Willy Jo is taking it real hard, giving himself all the blame. In my opinion, it's their daddy who's at fault. He ought to know his chances of making a farmer out of Bobby Dan are about as good as sneaking dawn past a rooster."

"Maybe he'll see that, now that both sons are away from home." Rosalie got up to put her sister's gloves away in her top drawer, mulling over all that had been shared. Tentatively, she turned to her sister. "I don't suppose Willy Jo sent any greetings for me—I mean, with all that was happening, it probably didn't cross his mind." At least, she hoped it hadn't. Talk of the Winthrops was stirring guilt over her growing friendship with Kenton.

"Willy Jo *did* send his greetings!"

Rosalie almost dreaded the words to come.

"He said, 'Give your sister my greetings.' That was his precise message."

Inwardly, Rosalie sighed with relief.

Vanda Mae paused but a second before delving with hushed enthusiasm into a new topic. "Now tell me about this

Mr. McCune. In your letters, you said he's a friend, but I think there's more to it than that."

"Vanda Mae!" Rosalie closed the bedroom door and began a long description of her association with Kenton that included the day he kept her from running away, their current efforts to trace the history of the infamous Cutler Gowen, and all the events in between.

~~~

Although Lottie and Benjamin had been required to report for a half day's work early the following Saturday morning, Rosalie was enjoying a later, unhurried meal with Kenton, her mother, and sister. She had devoted the previous two mornings to working with Kenton at his office while her sister and mother made acquaintance with the Doyle sisters. Kenton had wanted her to spend the entire day with her family, not just the afternoons, but she was too frustrated by lack of progress in tracking down Cutler Gowen's past to let that task go unattended. She broached the subject now with Kenton.

"What do you make of the letter that arrived yesterday from Mrs. Spicer saying her brother never knew anyone by the name of Cutler Gowen? If that's true, it seems mighty strange to me that Mr. Gowen himself referred to Lazarus Ambrose as his dearest friend."

Kenton set down his coffee cup. "Someone is obviously not telling the truth."

Rosalie's mother, who had been aghast to learn full details of the manner in which her brother and sister had been cheated out of their shop, said, "I can tell you who's lying. It's a good thing I've never met this Cutler Gowen. I'd be sorely tempted to wring his neck."

Vanda Mae's gaze settled on Rosalie. "What are you going to do next?"

Rosalie shrugged and turned to Kenton. "Yes, what *are* we going to do next?"

After a moment's thought, a smile crept over his face. "We're going to forget about Cutler Gowen and Lazarus Ambrose and take that ride out to the Reddicks' just like we promised Susan when we rang her up last night. I could do with a few hours in the country on a good riding horse."

Rosalie's mother smiled. "And I, the same." To Rosalie, she said, "No offense, dear, but after one day of euchre with Miss Ava and Miss Eda, and another day walking all about this fair city, I'm ready to climb aboard a good horse and ride."

To Rosalie, Vanda Mae said, "Be sure to put your knicker-bockers on beneath your skirt before we go. You never know when that ton of courage might come tumbling down on you."

Rosalie set her napkin aside. "I'll wear them, but don't get your hopes up. That ton of courage you've been praying for seems to be on an ounce-at-a-time delivery schedule."

~~~

On the drive to the Reddicks', Rosalie was unprepared for the enthusiastic manner in which her mother and sister spoke of her riding again. They seemed to assume that this time, it would really happen. Could she bear to disappoint them? Chills galloped up her spine, ending in bristled hairs on the back of her neck. Despite the warmth of the day—already seventy-five degrees by midmorning—her hands were cold and clammy, and the songs of the sparrows along the country road sounded more like a funeral dirge than a prelude to success.

The moment Kenton brought his carriage to a halt in the driveway, Susan and her father welcomed them. With introductions accomplished, Mr. Reddick led them toward the stable, his comments directed at Rosalie.

"Susan has taken the liberty of saddling up Penny for you."

The young girl said, "She's so tall, it'll be easiest to use the mounting platform to get on her." She indicated a wooden structure near the end of the building. "But Daddy and I will be right there to steady her and adjust your stirrups once you're in the saddle."

Inside the stable, Penny was cross tied in the aisle, all brushed, bridled, and saddled as had been promised. Standing there, outside of her stall, the horse suddenly seemed larger than Rosalie had remembered, and far more intimidating. Her heart began to flutter.

"I . . . I've changed my mind about riding today. Maybe some other time." She started to back away, but Vanda Mae prevented her, slipping her arm about her waist.

"I'm not going to let you run away this time, Sis. Penny is the perfect horse for you, I can tell just by looking at her. And you're going to get on her."

Mama stroked Penny's neck, giving her tack a cursory inspection. "Vanda Mae's right, Rosalie, Penny's a good choice, and getting on her will be easy as shoofly pie. You'll see."

John began unfastening the animal. "Like Susan said, we'll be right beside you every second. There's nothin' to worry about."

Despite the reassurances, Rosalie's mouth went dry. She wanted nothing more than to bolt out of the stable and away from the Reddick farm. Only Kenton's encouraging smile and her sister's firm hug kept her from doing so.

Mercifully, the mounting platform was situated beneath the shade of an oak. Vanda Mae led her up the steps. Now, looking down on the saddle, visions of her fall off Hurricane came rushing back. Vanda Mae, her mother, and Susan, encouraged her in turn.

"It's just one little step from here, Sis."

"There's no better time than now, to get on a horse again, dear."

"You can do it, Miss Foxe, just like I did!"

The longer Rosalie stood staring at the saddle, the more impossible the last step seemed.

Her mother grew impatient. "Don't keep the Reddicks and poor Penny waiting forever, dear. Just say a little prayer and lower yourself onto the saddle."

At her mother's suggestion, Rosalie's mind and body went numb. She needed time to expel the last of her fears and replace them with some frail semblance of confidence. Her mother's urgings seemed only to impede the process.

Kenton must have understood, for he took her mother by the elbow. "Mrs. Foxe, perhaps Rosalie will do better with fewer people looking on. Come, let me show you my pride and joy, my horse, Judge."

As he led her off toward the stable, she called over her shoulder, "You can do it, dear, I know you can!"

With her mother gone, Rosalie prayed for the fortitude to bend down, reach for the saddle horn, and settle herself on

Penny, but every last remnant of courage seemed to have taken flight like the sparrows.

CHAPTER 13

"Don't forget these!" Vanda Mae reminded Rosalie, holding up the knickerbockers she'd worn to the Reddicks' one week ago.

As Rosalie dressed to go downstairs for breakfast, she was dreading the visit they would soon make to the horse farm. Her fear of this day had plagued her all week long, giving her nightmares last night. By the time she'd crawled out of bed this morning, a butterfly ballet had begun in her stomach and she was incapable of stopping the performance.

Her sister and mother had made it perfectly clear all week long that they expected her to do more today than simply sit on Penny's back as she had done on her previous visit to the Reddicks'. The problem was, each time she envisioned herself actually riding a horse, Vanda Mae was riding horseback beside her, urging her on with words of courage and confidence. But her sister would not be allowed to mount a horse today.

Releasing an apprehensive sigh, Rosalie pulled the pant-like garment up beneath her skirt and stepped in front of the mirror. She was arranging the folds of blue serge over the knickerbockers when Vanda Mae came up behind her.

"You're going to do it today, Sis. You're going to ride Penny around the ring and nothing bad is going to happen."

Rosalie met Vanda Mae's gaze in the mirror. "I'd be a lot more sure of myself if you could ride beside me." Turning to face her sister, she admitted solemnly, "As it is, I'm so tied in knots, I'm not even sure I can manage to get in a saddle again."

"Oh, go on!" Vanda Mae offered an impetuous hug. She was releasing Rosalie when the sound of a buggy coming to a stop in front of the house caught their attention.

Vanda Mae hurried to the window, pushing back the curtain. "It's the Western Union hack."

Rosalie turned to the mirror again. "News for Kenton about Cutler Gowen, I hope. I'm more convinced every day that he sprang full-grown from behind a rock." She fussed with her hair, trying to tuck a loose strand into her topknot and finding little success.

Vanda Mae headed for the door. "I'm going down and find out." She returned moments later, a grin stretching the limits of her face as she shoved the telegram into Rosalie's hand. "This is the best news since Tassie had her foal!"

"Did Gaspar find Daddy's missing horses?" Rosalie wondered aloud. Focusing on the message addressed to Vanda Mae Foxe in care of Kenton McCune, she read, "'Permission granted to ride with Rosalie. Only. Letter to follow.'"

At her puzzled look, Vanda Mae quickly explained. "I wrote Daddy last week and told him you were considering riding again, and that I thought you'd be more likely to follow through if I could ride with you."

The butterflies in Rosalie's stomach seemed to be leaping across their stage in unison. "Now, you've done it, Vanda Mae! Now you've really put me on the spot!"

Vanda Mae wagged her finger. "Only a few minutes ago you told me you'd be more sure of yourself if I could ride with you. Well, you got your wish! Nothing's going to stop you, now!" Going straight to her trunk, Vanda Mae pulled out the riding breeches and shirt she'd brought north just in case, but hadn't bothered to unpack.

As Vanda Mae changed her clothes, the butterflies in Rosalie's stomach seemed to do one last leap before exiting the stage.

But as she learned an hour later when Kenton pulled into the Reddick's drive, the winged troupe had only taken an intermission. Now, they were back for the final act, and their performance was causing a minor case of nausea. Rosalie tried desperately to put her mind elsewhere—on the white clouds with their heavy grey bottoms portending rain before the day was through; on the skunk essence still lingering from a previous night's encounter with a foe; on the scolding of a blue jay and taunt of a grackle as a squirrel scurried over the branches of their old oak home. Still, her hands were cold and damp and her mouth dry and distasteful as though she'd been breakfasting on cotton batting.

As the carriage drew near the stable, Rosalie froze. Looking down at her left hand, she realized she was gripping the seat so tightly, her fingers had turned white. In desperation, she sent up a silent plea for help. *Dear Lord, send me courage, and send it now!*

She waited for her mother and sister to step out of the carriage before releasing her grip and allowing Kenton to help her down. His hand was warm and dry against her cool, damp one. His touch, and the smile of encouragement he offered, began to thaw her fears.

Somehow, she managed to make light conversation while the horses for Kenton and her mother were led from the stable, all saddled and ready. They mounted and rode off, then she and Mr. Reddick led Penny out of the stable followed by Susan and Vanda Mae, each atop chestnut mares. As Rosalie drew near the wooden mounting platform, a lesson from the Bible came to mind. She repeated it silently again and again and again. *I can do all things through Christ, I can do all things through Christ, I can do all things through Christ . . .*

The courage she had sought from God seemed to come a drop at a time, one for each step as she mounted the platform, and it fell far short of the dose needed to do what was expected of her. Stalled beside the huge horse, she was ready to abandon the scene when Vanda Mae's words penetrated the fear clouding her mind.

"Do this for yourself, Rosalie. You can, if you *want* to!"

Rooted in place, she tried to bend toward the horse, but could only remain stiff as a mannequin.

Her sister spoke again, this time in hushed words of prayer that floated to Rosalie on the soft summer breeze. "Dear Lord, my sister's a tad scared just now. Wrap her in a mantel of courage. Bind her fears and cast them out. Take her in your arms and set her on Penny's back, then carry her there until she knows no doubt or apprehension. In Jesus name, Amen."

Her movements no longer her own, Rosalie lowered herself onto Penny's back, took up the reins, and relaxed into the gentle jostling of the saddle, recalling after six long years the habit of moving with the horse's gait.

Having surmounted the toughest challenge, she managed to complete her first trip around the riding ring—led by Mr. Reddick and flanked by Susan and Vanda Mae—with no untoward results. Her courage building, she took the second trip around without his help, the younger girls keeping her fortitude intact. By the end of the hour, she was riding around the ring alone, a goal she'd assumed would require another week or two to accomplish.

The sense of satisfaction when showing Kenton and her mother her achievement made her wish she wouldn't have to wait a full eight days before repeating the experience, but the Reddicks were going away to a horse auction in Chicago and she wouldn't be able to ride Penny until next Sunday. Nevertheless, the glorious achievement buoyed her spirits all the way home. She was still elated when Mrs. Buckley met them at the door, a letter in her hand.

"Mr. McCune, this came for you special delivery not an hour ago. It's addressed to your office, but the postman brought it by thinking you'd like to have it before Monday morning."

Kenton quickly set his riding crop and helmet on the hall table. "Thank you, Mrs. Buckley."

With a nod, the hired woman retreated to her kitchen.

Rosalie studied the address over Kenton's shoulder. "It's from Mrs. Spicer."

Mama said, "I've been praying for news from out East."

"Please read it aloud, Mr. McCune," said Vanda Mae. "We all want to know what the woman has to say."

Removing the missive from the envelope, Kenton began. "'Dear Mr. McCune, I was visiting my dearly departed brother's grave a few days ago when I happened to read the inscription on an old headstone I had never noticed before. It says, "Cutler Gowen, born 1848, died 1872." At first, I thought the man in your city must be a descendant, but the granite marker made no mention of family, and I found no evidence of relatives buried near his grave site. My curiosity aroused, I searched records at the county office thinking I would find something about the man buried here that might shed light on the fellow by the same name in your city, perhaps information regarding a Cutler Gowen, Jr. Oddly enough, no birth or death records bearing the name "Cutler Gowen" can be located. The clerk said they are probably in the wrong file, but when I asked him to look more thoroughly, he became very irritated with me. I have an uneasy feeling about it that I cannot explain. I am asking around the city to see if anyone remembers Cutler Gowen, but so far, I have found none who knew him. Sorry I could not be of more help in the matter. If you think of any way in which I could be of further assistance, do not hesitate to ask. Sincerely, Mrs. Spicer.'"

Rosalie reached for the letter. "Do you think our Mr. Gowen is the son of this dead man?"

"Perhaps he's a nephew," said Mama.

"What are you going to do now, Mr. McCune?" Vanda Mae wanted to know.

In the thoughtful moment that followed, thunder rumbled over the bay. Taking the letter in hand again, Kenton said contemplatively, "I don't really know what I'll do, except to pray that Mrs. Spicer finds someone who knew Cutler Gowen and his kin."

~~~

In the wee hours of the morning, with the house dark and everyone sleeping to the patter of steady rain on the roof, Kenton lay awake, still thinking about the letter from Mrs. Spicer. He pondered again the conundrum of Cutler Gowen. Thunder cracked, then lightning flashed outside his window, momentarily illuminating the collection of photos occupying the table opposite his bed. Suddenly, a new thought bolted into his mind. Hopping out of bed, he hurriedly dressed, pulled on his Macintosh and galoshes, grabbed his umbrella from the hall stand, and made haste to the Western Union office. He was certain Mrs. Spicer could be of further assistance, and he wasn't about to waste a moment letting her know how.

In case his hunch proved false, he decided not to mention this communication to anyone lest he foster disappointments. Nevertheless, he could hardly wait for the woman's response.

CHAPTER 14

As Kenton drove home from his office the following Friday afternoon, he couldn't shake his disappointment at Mrs. Spicer's lack of response. He'd expected to hear from her before now, and was growing impatient. Even Rosalie noticed, adding she was glad he had given her two days off to take her mother and sister on an excursion to Northport aboard the *Columbia*. When she asked what was bothering him, he put her off. The wire sent East remained his secret.

He pulled into the carriage barn, unhitched and fed Nick, and had started for the house when he saw a postal delivery hack stop out front. He hurried to intercept the postman halfway up the front walk.

"Special Delivery for you, Mr. McCune. I missed you at your office and figured I ought to bring it by."

"I left a few minutes early today. Much obliged," Kenton said, his heart skipping a beat when he recognized Mrs. Spicer's handwriting. He was further encouraged by the stiffness and thickness of the envelope. Seeking a chair on the front porch, he heard Benjamin and Lottie in the parlor discussing their day at the candy factory as he ripped open the flap of the envelope and pulled out the contents.

A one-page letter enfolded two enclosures. He set it aside along with a news clipping, and stared down at the photograph of Mrs. Spicer's brother, Lazarus Ambrose. Kenton's blood rushed. He turned it over, finding the man's name and the date his picture was taken penned in Mrs. Spicer's hand. He set it aside to read the newspaper article, his mind spinning with the information contained therein. Finally, he read the letter. It opened with a brief statement that Lazarus Ambrose had died a loner without heirs. In the paragraphs that followed, Mrs. Spicer eulogized her honest, trustworthy, beloved late brother.

Kenton was still pondering all that he had discovered when Rosalie, Vanda Mae, and Mrs. Foxe came up the walk, singing a harmonious rendition of *Daisy Bell* in blended soprano voices. He rose from his chair to greet them as they climbed the porch steps.

"It's nice to see you're in such good spirits, ladies, and I have news that will make them even better!" He held up the envelope from Mrs. Spicer.

Rosalie, Mrs. Foxe, and Vanda Mae spoke in quick succession.

"Is our Cutler Gowen the son of the man in the cemetery?"

"Is he the nephew?"

"Tell us quick, Mr. McCune, before I expire of sheer curiosity!"

Kenton held the door open. "Come inside. I want Benjamin and Lottie to be in on this, too." In the parlor, he directed Rosalie to sit between her aunt and uncle on the sofa. Mrs. Foxe and Vanda Mae took chairs nearby.

Kenton pulled the portrait from the envelope and held it at eye level for Rosalie, her aunt, and uncle. "This is a photograph of Mrs. Spicer's brother, the late Lazarus Ambrose."

Lottie gasped, hands flying to her cheeks.

Ben scowled and mumbled under his breath.

Rosalie's mouth dropped open. She took the picture in hand to study it more closely, finally asking, "Do you think this could possibly be a fair-haired likeness of our dark-haired Cutler Gowen?"

With words quicker than logic, Vanda Mae said, "If it is, then Uncle Benjamin and Aunt Lottie are working for a dead man!"

Mrs. Foxe laughed. "Obviously not, but something's rotten as a basketful of spoiled eggs if the deceased Lazarus Ambrose has risen from the dead to live a second life as Cutler Gowen. Are you all certain the two are one and the same?"

Lottie studied the portrait a second time. "They *must* be."

"There's little doubt," said Benjamin.

"I think Mr. Gowen is using shoe polish on his hair to change his appearance," said Rosalie.

"There's more," said Kenton. "Mrs. Spicer sent a newspaper article that came out about a month after her brother's death. I'll read it to you." He perched on the edge of his winged chair. "'Embezzlement at New York Central. Accounts empty. Auditors at a loss to explain. A recent audit of accounts of the New York Central has revealed considerable irregularities. Banking deposits that were posted to the railroad's accounts were, in fact, never made. Railroad ledgers and bank books appear to have been falsified to cover the embezzlement of thousands of dollars. The exact amount is not known.

"'It is certain, however, that the late Lazarus Ambrose had charge of the accounts for the railroad. As you will recall, we reported in this newspaper one month ago that Mr. Ambrose was brutally murdered outside his Cherry Street home.

"'Mr. Ambrose was known by his fellow employees to have been meticulous with his bookkeeping. According to his supervisor at the Central, Mr. Ambrose's accounts were never out of balance in all the twenty years he was employed by the railroad.

"'Police fear that Mr. Ambrose stumbled on an embezzlement scheme and was killed before he could bring it to the attention of his superiors. Although they have thoroughly questioned employees at the Central and at the bank where the money was supposedly on deposit, they have no leads in the case."

Rosalie said, "It's obvious Mr. Gowen—Ambrose, or whatever his name is—used money he embezzled from the railroad out East to set up a candy factory here in Traverse City."

"He evidently assumed that by moving so far away, no one would discover his crime," said Mrs. Foxe.

Lottie leaned forward. "We must go to the Chief of Police immediately!"

Ben reached for the photograph. "I've a mind to take this straight to Mr. Gowen, shove it in his face, and see what he has to say!"

Kenton shook his head. "You'd better not."

"But he's a scoundrel! Stole huge sums of money! He must be called to account!"

His lawyer's mind taking over, Kenton warned, "But we haven't one iota of proof."

Mrs. Foxe focused on her brother. "He's one cunning critter, Benjamin, putting you out of your store the way he did.

The first instant he thinks someone's caught onto his ruse, he'll be off to parts unknown, never to be found again."

Vanda Mae sighed. "Lazarus Ambrose may have been an honest man when he was alive, but since he died, he certainly has proven himself to be one perfidious lout."

Kenton pondered aloud, "I wonder who's buried in Lazarus Ambrose's grave."

Lottie focused a squinted eye on him. "Do you think someone was murdered, maybe even by Mr. Ambrose, and was buried there instead of himself?"

Kenton shrugged. "It's impossible to say until the body is exhumed." After a moment's silence, he added, "And now that I think back on the death notice in Mr. Gowen's—or Ambrose's—wallet, it said that he had a closed-casket funeral."

Rosalie offered a wry smile. "That surely explains why Cutler Gowen called Lazarus Ambrose his very best friend."

Lottie chortled. "The best friend who made him wealthy."

Mrs. Foxe grew contemplative. "Poor Mrs. Spicer. She thinks her brother died an honest accountant. How will she take the news that he's alive and not . . ."

Kenton supplied the words, read from Mrs. Spicer's letter, "' . . .a gem of a man. Upright, honest, and completely devoted to the New York Central.' At least she won't have to know for awhile—not until investigations uncover enough proof of his secret criminal activities to warrant his arrest."

Rosalie spoke thoughtfully. "You'll have to send word to the police out East who investigated Ambrose's so-called murder and the embezzlement."

Kenton nodded. "I'll send a wire to the New York Central as well. They'll want to know of new leads in the case."

Lottie pondered the situation out loud. "I suppose this means we all have to go on treating Mr. Gowen as if nothing's changed."

Ben almost smiled. "Actors. We'll all be actors. Before you know it, we'll be appearing on stage at the Opera House."

Mrs. Foxe's head moved slowly from side to side. "I still can't help thinking of the shock Mrs. Spicer will suffer when she learns about her brother. There seems no easy way to apprise her of the truth."

Kenton said, "We'll cross that bridge when we come to it. In the meantime, we can pray for some merciful method of breaking the news."

~~~

Two days later, as Rosalie dressed to spend a Sunday afternoon horseback riding at the Reddicks', Vanda Mae observed her carefully. "You look every bit a horsewoman, dressed in the new riding breeches and boots you bought from Millikens yesterday—except for the worry lines on your forehead."

Rosalie sighed. "I thought I had conquered my fears, but the butterflies are back."

"Maybe they'll settle soon. Say, did I tell you? When Susan rang us up last night to invite us over, she said her daddy bought a new mare at the Chicago auction."

"You've mentioned it half a dozen times since last night."

"To hear Susan tell it, that new horse of hers is the finest mare this side of the Mason-Dixon line. I'd never say a word to disappoint her, but that mare can't be as nice as my April was."

"That's what you said last night," Rosalie reminded her.

Vanda Mae went on. "April was the finest riding horse I've ever seen. Daddy liked her so much, he—"

"—wanted to make her into a brood mare," Rosalie finished for her.

"I guess I told you that before, too."

Picking up her new riding gloves, Rosalie headed for the door. "If we don't get started soon, you'll have repeated your entire life's story before we get to the Reddicks', and it would be a pure shame to deprive Susan and her father of the pleasure of hearing it." She grinned.

"At least I got your mind off the butterflies and made the creases in your forehead disappear." Vanda Mae smiled broadly.

A quarter of an hour later, Kenton pulled into the Reddicks' drive. Susan, who was in the ring riding a chestnut horse, headed toward Kenton's rig. As she drew closer, Vanda Mae said, "That horse Susan is on is the same color as April. Her blaze is like April's too, the way it flares out on the right side. And look at her legs. She's got three white socks exactly like April."

The moment the buggy came to a halt, Vanda Mae jumped out and ran a few yards to the horse. "April, it's you!"

The mare nickered and bobbed her head.

Vanda Mae reached for her bridle, stroking her nose, then hugging her neck. "I found you, girl! I can hardly believe it! I found you!"

April nuzzled Vanda Mae's neck and let out a soft whinny.

Susan backed the horse away with a firm command, then addressed Vanda Mae. "What are you talking about? This is Queenie, *my* horse, the one Papa bought for me at Chicago!"

"But she was stolen from me earlier this month!" Vanda Mae insisted.

"We have the papers to prove this horse is ours!" Susan claimed.

The argument grew louder as Rosalie hurried to join the two girls, followed closely by Kenton, Mama, and Susan's father.

"Whoa, young ladies! What's this all about?" asked John.

With tears in her eyes, Susan turned to him. "Vanda Mae says Queenie is hers, that she was stolen, and we don't really own her. *Please* show her the paper that says we bought her, fair and square!"

Vanda Mae addressed her mother. "This is *April!* I'd know her anywhere! See the shape of her blaze, her three white socks, and the frost in her eyebrows?"

Mama took hold of April's bridle. She spoke softly to the animal, stroking her nose and inspecting her teeth and markings before turning to John. "My daughter's right, Mr. Reddick. My husband can prove this horse belongs to him, and she *was* stolen from us about three weeks ago."

John's expression hardened. "Then let your husband replevy the animal—put up security and take me to court." To Kenton, he said, "You'll represent me in this matter, won't you?"

Kenton seemed to look past him, at the stables in the distance, before focusing on his good friend. "I'm suffering from conflict of interest, being a family friend to both you and the Foxes. I'd be foolish to take either side in a dispute between you. But John, I'll give you this advice for free. If Mr. Foxe documents his ownership to the court's satisfaction, the animal will be returned to him."

Mama's gaze pinned John. "And there's no doubt in my mind, you'll lose."

Kenton rested a hand on John's shoulder. "From one friend to another, I believe your best recourse is to locate the fellow who brought the horse to auction."

John gazed at April, then at Susan, his blue eyes clouding over.

His daughter brushed away a tear with the back of her riding glove. "Don't let them take Queenie, Papa! You said yourself, she's just the mare we need to build up our stock and keep the place going."

He reached up, caressing Susan's moist cheek. "We've got to do what's right."

"I won't give her up! I *won't!*" The young girl dug her heels into April's flanks and rode off in a cloud of dust.

Rosalie spoke up as the air cleared. "Mr. Reddick, I'll be glad to type up a letter from Mr. McCune to the auction house informing them that they've been party to traffic in stolen property and inquiring as to the seller's whereabouts. It might help you recover your investment so you can purchase some other animal."

"Something must be done to catch the thief, and the sooner, the better," said Mama.

A hand shading her eyes, Vanda Mae watched Susan and April disappear across a wide meadow and into the adjoining woods. "One thing's certain, I've just lost my hankering for a horseback ride. Maybe Mr. McCune should take us straight to his office so Rosalie can use his typing machine."

Mama nodded. "And we should wire my husband about April."

"I'd be much obliged for the help," said John, "but I don't think it'll make a difference. If the horse was stolen, the thief'd be long gone from Chicago by now."

"'Nothing venture, nothing win,' William Gilbert, *Iolanthe,* Act II," said Kenton. "If you'll fetch the address of the auction house and the papers on the horse, the Foxe ladies and I will post a letter before the day is through."

CHAPTER 15

As Kenton pulled off the road at a scenic lookout a few miles north of the city on the Mission Peninsula, Rosalie was thankful that he'd suggested the Sunday afternoon drive as an alternative to the horseback riding plans that had fallen through at the Reddicks'. This was her first carriage ride on the strip of land that separated the west side of Grand Traverse Bay from the east, and she was pleased that her mother and sister seemed to be enjoying the outing as much as she was. With pastoral views to the east and watery vistas to the west, thoughts of the letter they had posted to the Chicago auction house earlier that afternoon took flight.

Her entire attention was now on the visual delights surrounding her, as well as the scented ones, for the road was trimmed with a heavily perfumed, pink edging of phlox. She wanted to enjoy the moment fully, for one day soon she would be aboard a train heading home with her mother and sister so that Vanda Mae could start school at Salem Academy on the fifth of September.

Standing on the sandy shore, she gazed at the rippled expanse of blue dotted by white triangles, and relished the warm breeze. Too soon, she would be heading south. Little by little, she'd grown accustomed to Grand Traverse Bay and the Queen City on its shore, and she now had grown fond of the region—and fonder yet of the man beside her who called it his home.

She ventured a furtive glance at Kenton. He was looking in the direction of Bassett Island, a sand-rimmed patch of green a short distance offshore, but his gaze seemed to go beyond the tiny isle. What thoughts gave him such a faraway look? He turned to her, his brow creased.

"I hope I'm not speaking out of turn, but I've been thinking." His focus now taking in her mother, he continued. "Mrs. Foxe, would you consider permitting your eldest daughter to remain longer in Traverse City?" To Rosalie, he said, "That is, if it's agreeable to you. I still need your help with the Gowen case, and there's the new problem over the Morgan, as well as my regular work load and—"

Vanda Mae interrupted. "Sis, you've got to stay!"

Rosalie's tongue froze.

"It's up to you, dear," said Mama.

Rosalie turned to Kenton, her heart far lighter than just moments ago. But she kept her smile modest and her answer simple. "I'll stay."

Vanda Mae beamed. "Good! It's settled!"

~~~

Rosalie's sense of elation was with her still when she laid her head on her pillow that night. For a while longer, she could linger in the home of the man for whom she'd developed a real fondness, and continue to assist him daily at his office. But a troubling question lurked in her mind. Was she only postponing the inevitable, making it harder to part when the time came? She sent up a quick prayer.

"Father in Heaven, guide me in the path you would have me take, and in my feelings for those around me, especially where Mr. McCune is concerned. In Jesus' name, Amen."

Though a sense of peace washed over her, a new concern arose—that Susan Reddick's recently acquired horse was rightfully the possession of Vanda Mae. The young Reddick girl's words repeated in her mind, words she had quoted from her father . . . *she's just the mare we need to build up our stock and keep the place going* . . . an indication that John Reddick was struggling still.

On the heels of that thought came the prayer she'd said weeks ago on John's behalf, asking the Lord to provide his need. She'd thought the answer had come the day of the circus when Susan had recovered Cutler Gowen's money clip and earned a $200 reward for her good deed. A question now hit her like a bolt from heaven—was Vanda Mae's horse another answer to that prayer?

Rosalie had never expected her sister to suffer because of it. Logically, she could easily conclude that April's appearance at the Reddick farm was strictly coincidence. From deep within, she had to ask herself if coincidence was really the case, or if Divine intervention provided a truer definition for the strange circumstances?

Prayer seemed the only hope for answers. She quietly asked the Lord to guide her in her search for the horse thief, and to give all involved in the matter both the wisdom and the grace to recognize and accept his will.

Moments later, she fell into a pleasant dreamland that was not only free from worry over April, but filled with images of her pleasant afternoon by the bay and the man who had made them memorable.

~~~

Six days later, as Kenton drove home from the Boston Store sale, Rosalie could barely see above the boxes and paper-wrapped packages stacked on her lap. Beside her on the rear seat of the carriage, her mother and sister were equally laden with purchases. Rosalie chuckled to herself, thinking it was so like her mother to postpone her departure for Tanglewood by a day in order to take advantage of the Saturday bargains offered in the newspaper ad.

For Rosalie and Vanda Mae, Mama had purchased silk waists reduced from $8 to $2.48. For Papa, she found an umbrella reduced from fifty cents to twenty-nine cents, and several ties for a quarter apiece—half their regular price. For herself, she had purchased four-yard lengths of silk at fifty-nine cents a yard—down from a dollar—and dozens of one-, two-, three-, and five-cent values including Valenciennes lace, a curling iron, darning cotton, handkerchiefs, embroidery floss, buttermilk and almond meal soap, white pearl buttons, and other notions. The trick now would be to fit everything into their trunks and onto the train. But somehow, her mother would manage.

Now, as Kenton turned onto Washington Street, Rosalie's mind turned to other thoughts as well. Despite the distraction of the shopping trip, it was clear that Kenton was troubled by the lack of response from both the police department in Rochester and the New York Central Railroad regarding his speculation that Lazarus Ambrose was likely operating under the alias of Cutler Gowen. He was concerned, too, that the auction house in Chicago had been quick to deny any indiscretion regarding the sale of the Morgan to John Reddick, and had refused to divulge the name and address of the former owner. She hated to see her own father and Susan's in a court fight over the animal, and prayed again that the Lord's will would be done.

When Kenton pulled into the driveway and helped her down from the carriage, she shoved troubling thoughts aside. Despite legal challenges and worries, she was still pleased that she would be remaining in his company for the weeks to come.

This notion was dislodged, however, by the sound of a stranger's voice—a male voice—which was flowing from the parlor window, and the quiet tone of her mother when she alighted from the carriage.

Mama cocked her head, pausing to listen to Lottie's cascade of chuckles and Ben's quiet laughter in response to something the fellow had said. "Mr. McCune, it seems a gentleman has come calling. An acquaintance of yours, perhaps?"

Kenton listened to more of the congenial masculine tones and feminine laughter. "I don't recognize the voice, but from the sound of it, he's a friend of your sister and brother."

With an inquisitive little smile, Mama lifted her skirt and stepped off toward the front porch. Rosalie and Vanda Mae followed her into the house, leaving Kenton to put away his rig and see to the packages.

In the front parlor, Ben occupied the couch and Lottie the love seat, her attention focused on the gentleman who amply filled the chair beside her. His round cheeks were pink with joviality, and he rose the moment the women entered the room.

Lottie made introductions. "Ladies, this is Detective O'Shea, come all the way from the police department in Rochester, New York to investigate Mr. Gowen. Detective O'Shea, meet my sister, Mrs. Fergus Foxe, and her daughters, Rosalie and Vanda Mae, from North Carolina."

His blue eyes sparkled beneath dark, thick brows. "My, my! A right pretty bouquet of southern roses you ladies make!"

Mama smiled. "Thank you, sir!" She took a seat beside her sister. While Rosalie and Vanda Mae settled on the couch beside their uncle, Mama continued. "Now that you're here, Detective, I truly hope you won't waste any time arresting that awful Cutler Gowen—or Lazarus Ambrose, as he was evidently known in your neck of the woods."

Lottie spoke up. "The detective wants to talk with Kenton first."

Ben rose. "I'll go out and tell him Detective O'Shea is waiting to see him."

While he was gone, Lottie explained that the detective had taken a room next door with the Doyle sisters. When he'd asked directions to Kenton's office, they'd brought him to Kenton's home, and in his absence, had introduced him to her and Ben, leaving the policeman there to await Kenton's return.

A few minutes later, Kenton shook the detective's hand, then reviewed the information he'd obtained which had prompted him to send a telegram to the Rochester Police Department, including the newspaper clipping and photograph from Mrs. Spicer. Detective O'Shea pulled Kenton's missive from his pocket and tapped it on his palm.

"This sent me on a course straight to the New York Central authorities. They obliged me with train tickets to Michigan, but we've a long way to go, collecting evidence, before an arrest can be made. First, I need to get a look at Cutler Gowen myself and make a determination if he's actually Lazarus Ambrose, like you think."

"The two men were acquaintances back East," said Ben, "so Detective O'Shea can't be seen by Gowen in the process."

"If he *is* Lazarus Ambose" said Lottie, "you can get Police Chief Rennie to help make the arrest so you can take him back to New York for his trial."

O'Shea chuckled. "Whoa, lass! You're gettin' the cart way out front of the pony. Like the newspaper said, we investigated about a month after his so-called death when certain accounts came up empty, but we couldn't get to the bottom of it. If the man truly is alive and not buried in his grave, we've got to find out who or what lies in his coffin and proceed from there."

"All without his sister growing suspicious," said Kenton. "She still visits his grave, you know."

Mama nodded. "She'll be mighty upset if you don't allow her sainted brother to rest in peace."

The detective gave a wink. "God forgive me if I tell dear Mrs. Spicer that we've discovered new information about her brother's murderer and need to examine his poor, mutilated body once more before making an arrest."

Vanda Mae spoke up. "Since Lazarus Ambrose killed himself, you won't be fibbing."

Rosalie added, "You just won't be telling her everything you know—for her own good."

The detective raised a pudgy finger. "First things first. I've got to get a good look at the fellow."

"His office at the factory has a big window to the right of the front door," said Ben. "You could come there Monday morning, about nine, and take a peek."

Lottie shook her head. "Monday is Labor Day, Ben. Everyone will be at the parade, but I have an idea. Mr. Gowen is already planning to drive his fancy wagon down the center of Front Street with Miss Hackbardt playing Candy Queen like she did on the Fourth. Detective O'Shea would be just another face in the crowd."

Mention of Clarissa stirred latent curiosity in Rosalie. "I'm still befoggled by the missing coin. That Hackbardt woman has got to have it somewhere."

O'Shea's brow twitched. "Missing coin?"

Kenton appeared on the brink of a reply when the sound of Miss Eda's voice floated through the front screen door. "Hello? Mr. McCune? Detective O'Shea?"

Their answer brought her to the front parlor where her gaze took in the entire company.

"I've come to invite you all to supper with Ava and me and our newest guest." She beamed at the detective. "I'm sure you could use more time with Mr. McCune."

O'Shea nodded. "He owes me an explanation about a missing coin." He turned to Kenton. "How about it, Mr. McCune? Would you be willing to divulge your information over dinner next door?"

Kenton's brow furrowed.

Before he could answer, Lottie spoke up. "I see no reason not to. With Mrs. Buckley away on her night off, this is the perfect opportunity for us to gather around the Doyles' table. Miss Eda, we'll be glad to accept your invitation, providing you allow me and my kin to help you get the meal on."

~~~

At supper, Rosalie couldn't help noticing certain amicable looks passing between Detective O'Shea and Lottie, who was seated directly across from him. When the Rochester native had dug into his potato salad and ham and delivered profuse compliments to his hosts, he again raised the question of the missing coin. Kenton wisely suggested Rosalie's aunt fill him in on the details. Lottie's explanation of the purloined double eagle and her frequent mention of Cutler Gowen's name in conjunction with Clarissa Hackbardt's, brought a thoughtful look to the detective's brow. He listened to the complete story, then replied.

"You were tellin' of a parade on Monday where I might get a good look at this fellow, drivin' his candy wagon."

Lottie nodded. "Just remember, he's blackened his hair since he was Lazarus Ambrose."

O'Shea grinned. "His color 'o hair won't fool me. I *would* like to get a close look at him. Hear the sound of his voice."

"How can you do that without being recognized, yourself?" Rosalie asked.

Eda dabbed the corners of her mouth with her napkin. "You must be careful. It'd be a shame to spoil things, when you've come so far."

Ava blinked rapidly. "It most assuredly would. If only we could help you somehow . . ."

The detective's blue eyes twinkled. "I've a plan, a notion clever as a leprechaun's. But I'll need plenty o' help 'tween now and the top o' Monday mornin' to carry it off."

Detective O'Shea described his secret hobby. Even in Rochester, few people aside from his brothers and sisters knew that the lifelong bachelor spent many an off-duty Saturday, and each and every parade day, playing the part of a clown, his greatest joy being to make children laugh.

In Michigan, however, he had none of his clown paraphernalia—no costume, no make-up, no props. And even if he'd brought them, which had never crossed his mind, he'd have been unable to use them since Lazarus Ambrose could recognize him as the clown from the Rochester parades, thus growing suspicious.

So the detective proposed that he dress himself as a different clown character from the one he portrayed back East. From Kenton, he solicited an old jacket that was several sizes too small, stretching ridiculously over his ample belly. From Ben, whose feet were nearly the same size as his own, he borrowed an old pair of shoes that could be painted white with bright red and yellow spots.

Ben supplied him, too, with a pair of white pants—the type worn by a candy maker—and Ava and Eda offered to sew bright red and yellow trim on his pants and jacket.

As for his head, Rosalie and her aunt fashioned a red yarn wig. And Vanda Mae loaned him her straw boater. The too-small hat, perched on top of the yarn hair, lent the right touch of whimsy to the developing character.

Work was progressing well on the detective's costume by the time Rosalie kissed her mother and sister good-bye at the depot early Sunday. By late that afternoon, the clown costume was in readiness except for the shoes, which still needed paint. Some spirit gum and putty was also needed to fashion a large round nose, and Detective O'Shea desperately needed balloons in red, white, and yellow, and long, thin sticks to tie them to.

At four o'clock, Rosalie accompanied Kenton on a mission to obtain the missing items from Wilhelms' Mercantile, looking the shopkeeper up at his home. A trip to the store, normally closed on Sundays, provided the coveted necessities, and an evening of blowing up balloons resulted in a huge, colorful bouquet.

Early Monday morning, following Detective O'Shea's directions, Rosalie assisted her aunt and the Doyle sisters in concocting clown make-up from common pantry ingredients. She then watched in awe as the jolly Irishman transformed his facial features.

He began by applying large patches of white about his eyes, covering his eyelids as well. Another patch of white rimmed his lower lip and chin. When the white had been powdered down, he applied pink to the remaining areas of his face and neck. Then, with great skill, he began outlining with a thin brush. First, red was applied to exaggerate his mouth. Then, black was used. With it, the detective first rimmed his white eye patches and added laugh lines. He then turned his ordinary mustache into a handlebar. And lastly, he outlined the white surrounding his chin. When he had finished, he applied his bulbous red nose.

Minutes later, in full costume, he took up his bouquet of balloons and stood in the center of the parlor for all to admire his completed costume.

Lottie's head moved from side to side. "I'd never recognize you, Detective O'Shea."

"I'm Freddy, the Clown!" His painted-on smile broadened.

Ben gave him a good looking-over. "Freddy, if I hadn't seen for myself, I'd never have known you and the detective are one and the same."

"Cutler Gowen, or Lazarus Ambrose, whichever he is, will never know you, either," said Rosalie.

Kenton and the Doyle sisters concurred.

To Kenton, O'Shea said, "I'd like to get to the startin' point o' the parade plenty early—get a close look at this candy man, hear him talkin' before he rolls down the street atop his wagon."

Kenton checked his watch. "We can go now, if you like."

The detective nodded, then approached Lottie, lifting feet and elbows high in clownish exaggeration. "Miss Marshall, when I see you at the parade, I'll be givin' you a balloon— white if our suspect's not Lazarus Ambrose, red if he is."

Solemnly, she replied, "I'll be praying for a red balloon, Freddy."

Tipping his hat, he turned and headed out the door, his comic clown walk leaving Rosalie, Lottie, and the Doyle sisters laughing.

CHAPTER 16

Nearly two and a half months had passed since the Labor Day Parade. Traverse City was quieter, and a good bit cooler than it had been on that last holiday of the summer season. But Rosalie couldn't ride down Front Street with Kenton even now, on the second Sunday in November, without recalling the moment Detective O'Shea in his "Freddy, the Clown" costume had walked up to Lottie. One foot after the other lifted high, he paused and handed her not one, but *three* red balloons.

As Kenton drove past the American Candy Company factory and out of town toward the Reddicks', Rosalie wondered why no effort had been made to arrest the notorious Lazarus Ambrose, alias Cutler Gowen. The detective had warned before departing for Rochester that he would need time to develop a solid case against all those he suspected of being involved in embezzlement from the New York Central, but she hadn't expected more than two months to pass without a word from the jolly Irishman.

Such thoughts troubled her, as did her curiosity over Kenton's out-of-town trip this past week. He'd told no one of his destination, nor the exact day of his return. When she'd asked if he was headed to Rochester, he'd only smiled. At least, when he arrived home four days later, he was in excellent humor, though tired.

She was silently speculating on what might have transpired during Kenton's sojourn when he pulled into Reddicks' drive for the horseback ride the two of them had planned for the afternoon. They had already chosen a route, one that would take them to a high hill on another road south of town. There, Kenton promised her an impressive view of West Bay and the Mission Peninsula. But when he turned to her, a look of skepticism in his hazel eyes told her even before his words did, that he was again pondering a question he'd already asked her five times in the previous twenty-four hours.

"Are you *sure* you want me to return Nick to the Reddicks and go back to driving Judge?"

"I'm sure!" Though she was certain of her own confidence in the grey horse, established gradually over the past two months of regularly riding Penny alongside Kenton and Judge, the lawyer side of Kenton evidently couldn't resist one last opportunity to cross-examine her.

Thoughts of Penny and Judge took flight when Rosalie noticed Susan atop April in the riding ring at the end of the driveway. The young girl paused to wave hello, then continued with her training routine.

"Every time I see that young lady with April," said Rosalie, "I'm thankful Daddy had the wisdom not to press claim to her."

Kenton smiled. "He saved several friendships and a horse farm by purchasing Vanda Mae a new mare, instead."

His comment provoked a question. "Did I tell you, she and Susan are sharing stories about April and Topaz through the mail?"

Kenton chuckled. "A few times."

"It's hard to believe Vanda Mae nearly lost Topaz to that horse thief, too. Willy Jo must know he's worth his weight in wildcats for catching the bandits."

~~~

Mention of Rosalie's North Carolina friend ignited a flicker of jealousy within Kenton, one he squelched quickly as he parked his rig outside the stable and focused on their purpose at hand. "Enough about the Morgans. Let's go get Penny and Judge. John's probably got them saddled and waiting inside."

Half an hour later, having told John where they were headed and when to expect their return, they cantered into the hilly region south of town. Kenton kept Rosalie on his right to cushion her from oncoming traffic. At least, that's what he told her, but he had other reasons. He loved to watch her while she watched the countryside. He loved the way the breeze blew tendrils of her hair loose from the little felt hat that was perched on her head. He loved the way her grey wool riding habit fluttered about her ankles. And he especially loved the way she sat erect and confident upon her side-saddle, a skill she had acquired through dedication and training these last several weeks.

The fact that she was on a horse at all made him proud enough to crow, but he kept a tight lid on such emotions. Her confidence and her form had improved so much from that first day when she had tentatively mounted Penny, he needed to remind himself she was the same person. For a woman who had refused to get on a horse for six years, she was now riding beside him as if she'd been born to it. She appeared as if she'd never fallen in her life, nor suffered from a crippled right arm, and he couldn't help but admire her for it.

Of course, that wasn't all he had come to admire in this young miss from North Carolina. He anticipated the start of each and every day, hearing her mild southern drawl, which was softening with her tenure in the North. And he enjoyed working with her in his office. Her schooling at Salem Academy had provided a solid education, and with a dogged tenacity, she had mastered typewriting and stenography better than others not challenged by an imperfect right arm.

Nearing the lookout, he pulled ahead, leading her off the main road along a winding path to a higher hill that peaked in a lookout over the bay. He dismounted, then held Penny steady for Rosalie to do the same. They stood side by side in silence, each taking in the panorama of blue-grey waters bound at the bottom by a small jewel of a city, and on its sides by land made barren in preparation for winter snows.

Wind rustled through the brown meadow grass at their feet, and far off, a train whistle blew. The haunting sound served as a reminder that Rosalie would soon be on her way home to Tanglewood for Thanksgiving. The thought dampened his spirits. After five months of having her near, he was unwilling to let her go, even though she planned to return immediately after the holiday and stay in Michigan through Christmas and the New Year.

But supposing she changed her mind? Her old friend and neighbor, Willy Jo, would undoubtedly be very much in evidence. He could influence her to see out the year down South.

Feeling possessive and protective, Kenton slipped his arm about Rosalie's waist and drew her firmly to his side.

The startled look that met him transformed instantly to a questioning smile, but he made no comment, letting silence reign as she relaxed against him, her head on his shoulder, her sweet essence of peach blossoms comforting him.

~~~

Rosalie savored the new closeness Kenton offered. She could only guess at the reason for his sudden show of affection, and the uncharacteristic worried look in his eyes. It was not unlike the troubled waters of the bay, growing greyer with foreboding as dark clouds built in, precursors of a storm to come. Perhaps Kenton's concern was caused by the same thoughts that distracted her more frequently as each day passed—the knowledge that she would soon be departing for North Carolina—though temporarily.

In many ways, she was not looking forward to another separation. Reluctant as she had been to remain in the North five months ago, she was now equally reluctant to head south. Kenton's brief trip out of town had made her realize he'd come to mean more to her than simply a lawyer who had negotiated passage through the difficult straits of foreclosure. More, too than an employer who had invited her to sail with him daily on the challenging waters of a city law practice. He had become her special friend, patient and strong enough to guide her past her fear of horses just as he was guided himself by a firm faith in the Lord. His routine of attending worship services each Sunday morning was more than an outward habit. Rosalie knew Kenton well enough after all these months to understand that he carried the Lord in his heart all the week through.

In fact, the more she knew of Kenton, the more remarkable she found him. Who else would have bought a home just to share it with friends who were in need? He had made light of the gesture, claiming he'd done it for Ben and Lottie because they were like family—the kindest folks he'd known since leaving the orphanage family represented in the photographs in his room. Nevertheless, Rosalie considered him wonderfully magnanimous.

She admired his generosity toward one particular motherless girl, as well. That Susan Reddick idolized him was both understandable and justified. He had shown true Christian love, seeing Susan through the trauma of a broken leg and the challenges of riding again, and helping with her mother's needs. And his caring hadn't stopped there. He'd been willing—even eager—to spend the day with her at the circus, an experience her father would never have provided. Surely, the many kindnesses Kenton had shown clearly indicated that his capacity for love and affection ran deep and abundant.

And the tenderness he was showing her now, holding her close, spoke subtly of his feelings for her where words remained unsaid. How she wanted to tell him that she had grown to care for him more than she had ever thought possible, but she dared not utter a word of such sentiments now. She dared not assume such feelings were mutual. When the time was right, she was certain they would express their true regard for one another. For now, it was enough to stand close, to lean on his strength and support. She could stay here forever, indulging the new sensation and studying the scenic view, but the sound of hooves wending up the hill caused them to part.

CHAPTER 17

"Mr. McCune? Miss Foxe? Are you there?" Susan's voice preceded her to the lookout.

"Up here, Susan," Kenton quickly responded.

She emerged atop April, her expression a picture of excitement. "Mr. Marshall rang up. He said you're to return home immediately. Mr. Gowen has been arrested and the authorities want to talk to you!"

Rosalie gasped, her heart rushing.

Kenton beamed at her, impulsively kissing her on the cheek. "Let's go! This is what we've been waiting for!"

Susan followed Rosalie and Kenton to his house at a gallop. Once there, she offered to take their horses to her father's stable and return with Judge and his rig.

Kenton ushered Rosalie inside. No sooner had they entered the foyer than Detective O'Shea hustled forth from the parlor to greet them.

"There ye be! Come! My associate is more than eager to see you!" He nudged Rosalie toward the parlor, pausing momentarily to confer in whispers with Kenton.

In the parlor, Lottie introduced Rosalie to the silver-haired representative from the New York Central, Lawrence Lyons, who unfolded his long legs and rose from the sofa to shake her hand. She was vaguely aware that Kenton acknowledged previous acquaintance with the man from his secretive out-of-town trip only days before.

Her attention had been greatly distracted by the woman sitting beside Lyons—Clarissa Hackbardt—looking for all the world like the cat who swallowed the canary.

Rosalie narrowed her gaze on her nemesis. "What are *you* doing here?"

"Miss Hackbardt helped Detective O'Shea get the evidence he needed to arrest Mr. Gowen," said Lottie, taking a place beside Ben on the love seat.

Clarissa held up a bank draft. "And as you can see, I've been amply rewarded for my efforts."

Rosalie read the figure on the check, nearly choking at the generous amount. "You don't deserve a penny of that money! You're nothing but a devious, deceitful—"

Ben interrupted. "Rosalie, enough! Mr. Lyons has other business to discuss."

Lottie motioned to the pair of unoccupied wing chairs. "You and Mr. McCune make yourselves comfortable. Mr. Lyons assures us we'll like what he's about to say, now that we're all here."

Barely holding her tongue in check, Rosalie did as she was asked. Seated beside her, Kenton reached for her hand, giving a reassuring squeeze while Mr. Lyons focused his attention on Ben and Lottie.

"Now that Mr. Gowen and his twelve accomplices in Rochester are under lock and key, Mr. Depew—Chauncey Depew, that is, head of the New York Central—has authorized me to award temporary possession of the American Candy

Company factory and store to you, Mr. Benjamin and Miss Lottie Marshall, such possession to become permanent pending the outcome of Lazarus Ambrose's trial."

"And guilty, he'll be found," said O'Shea. "We've way more than enough evidence to be assured o' that." He glanced Clarissa's way, bringing a smug smile to her face that soured Rosalie's stomach and squelched satisfaction over the good news.

Lottie turned to Ben, her forehead wrinkled with unasked questions.

He adjusted his glasses and gave a little shake of his head. "Did I hear you right? My sister and I are to own the store, *and* the factory?"

Lyons nodded, slipping two sets of identical papers from the portfolio at his feet. He handed one to Ben and Lottie, the other to Kenton, which he shared with Rosalie. Still addressing the Marshalls, Lyons said, "Your attorney, Mr. McCune, here, is the toughest, most philanthropic negotiator I've ever come up against in all my experiences at the New York Central."

Rosalie spoke up. "Begging your pardon, sir, but the two words don't seem to describe the man I know. Mr. McCune has shown no end to his kind and generous nature, but tough?"

A wry smile tilted the railroad official's mouth. "At the Central, we were willing to grant that Mr. McCune was entitled to a reward for discovering the whereabouts of Mr. Ambrose. Especially considering the vast sums he embezzled and our recent recovery of the majority of them. But no lawyer has ever been granted terms that would result in ownership of an entire factory and retail establishment, then insisted the properties be put in the names of his friends!"

Rosalie held tight to Kenton's hand, her heart soaring as she absorbed the meaning of Mr. Lyons' words, and the grateful smiles they brought to her aunt's and uncle's faces.

To Kenton, Lyons said, "Mr. Depew, himself, approved the terms you demanded when we met in Rochester earlier this week. The agreement is all laid out here, requiring only the signatures of your clients, Benjamin and Lottie Marshall, and a small token showing their desire to retain permanent possession of the businesses when Ambrose has been convicted." To Ben and Lottie, he explained further.

"Mr. Depew is delighted to make you the owners of the shop and factory—provided you don't intend to simply sell them at the first opportunity. He's a firm advocate of longevity in business in the Vanderbilt tradition."

Rosalie and Kenton read the papers in silence until the very last line, which she read a second time, out loud. "'This agreement shall be in force upon payment of one twenty-dollar gold piece by Benjamin and Lottie Marshall, and signatures of same.'"

Lyons explained. "You have to understand Mr. Depew. He has a penchant for sealing agreements with the exchange of a gold coin. In this case, he's specified a double eagle."

Ben turned his pockets inside out and searched through a fistful of coins, finding only pennies, nickels, dimes, and a half dollar. "Wouldn't you know. For want of a double eagle, a candy store and factory are lost."

Rosalie's heart sank. "Surely you must have some money tucked away upstairs."

Lottie's joyful look began to fade. "We don't usually keep such valuables in our apartment, but I'll look."

While she was upstairs, Detective O'Shea described the events that had unfolded in the past two months including Kenton's visit as the investigation was nearing its close, and the arrest of the twelve accomplices to Lazarus Ambrose's elaborate scheme, from the coroner to the undertaker to the bank teller—even a member of the police department.

"Mr. Ambrose was the mastermind, the others were his disciples, and a cunning lot they were. But we got them all, and most of the money they'd swindled. But we'd 've gotten nary a one if Mr. McCune hadn't put us on the right track, so to speak!" He winked.

Lottie returned from upstairs, her brow troubled. "I was right. I deposited all but a few silver dollars in the bank two days ago."

Kenton reached deep into his own pockets, a strange look passing between him and O'Shea as he did. Producing a money clip of bills and half a dozen small coins, Kenton said, "Sorry I can't help. Perhaps we can postpone execution of the agreement until tomorrow morning when the bank opens."

Lyons shook his head. "I'm leaving on the first train out tomorrow. If we don't act on this today, the operation of the candy factory and shop will have to cease until such time as I can return, two weeks or more from now."

Detective O'Shea's sunny humor flagged. "Such a shame to put so many good people out o' work with the holidays comin' on, and all." He turned in earnest to Clarissa. "Miss Hackbardt, you've been God's own blessin' to me and Mr. Lyons in this case. Might there be the least little chance you or someone you know would have a double eagle to lend?"

She smiled graciously. "Allow me." Bending down, she reached beneath the hem of her navy serge skirt to remove her *left* shoe, plucking from it a shiny double eagle.

Rosalie shot out of her chair. "Let me see that!" Snatching the coin away, she immediately recognized the nick in the edge near the word "God" in the phrase, "In God We Trust." So Clarissa had kept the coin hidden in her *left* shoe all along, not the *right* shoe as Rosalie had suspected the night of the ball last July. Her heart pounded.

"You stole this! It's the exact same coin I paid you against Aunt Lottie and Uncle Benjamin's mortgage last summer. You took it just so Mr. Gowen—Ambrose—could repossess the store!"

"I did *not* steal that coin!" she asserted. "But even if I *had,* your aunt and uncle would be much better off paying for an entire factory and shop with it today, than if they'd made one month's payment on the candy store last summer."

Rosalie grew adamant. "You stole it! You stole it and caused all manner of upset, and I won't let you get away—"

Kenton intervened, his words resolute. "Miss Foxe! In the interest of sealing the agreement with Mr. Lyons and the New York Central, we must postpone this argument until another time."

Piqued at Kenton and frustrated beyond words, Rosalie sat down and folded her arms against her chest.

When signatures had been witnessed on both copies of the original agreement and the controversial coin placed in the possession of Mr. Lyons, Lottie favored Clarissa with a puzzled smile.

"Miss Hackbardt, I'd be most grateful if you could explain something. After Mr. Gowen put us out of home and business, why did he offer us good jobs and part ownership of this beautiful home?"

She chuckled. "Mr. McCune convinced him he'd never really succeed in the candy business in this city unless he added *your* fudge and chocolates to his line of confections. Then he told Lazarus what it would cost, and assured him that if he didn't have you on his payroll, you'd be back in business with someone else, stealing the bulk of the candy trade." With a fleeting glance at Mr. Lyons, she continued. "At the railroad, Lazarus learned the importance of eliminating the competition. 'The way of the Vanderbilts,' he's fond of saying. Lazarus put you *out* of business to establish his monopoly. He *hired* you to guarantee its future."

Ben scratched his chin. "That explains our jobs and our fudge recipe. What about our share in this house?"

Bestowing a grudging look of admiration on Kenton, Clarissa then focused on Ben. "Lazarus says your lawyer is the only person he's ever encountered who caused him to suffer a temporary lapse of greed."

Kenton turned to Clarissa. "And what about you, Miss Hackbardt?" He stood and began to pace, hands linked behind him. When he spoke again, his tone changed from friendly, to a cold, inquisitive nature Rosalie had never heard from him before.

"No one has ever caused you to suffer a temporary lapse of greed, have they, Miss Hackbardt? No one, that is, until Detective O'Shea, a few moments ago, when he convinced you to produce that double eagle. It *is* the one Miss Foxe paid you for her aunt and uncle's mortgage last June the twenty-ninth, *isn't it?*" He paused to stare at her.

Pinned beneath his cold, condemning gaze, Clarissa lowered her head, then faced him again with renewed conviction. "The ledger book in Lazarus's office proves that payment was never made!"

"That's a *false* ledger book! One you made up to omit record of payment!"

A flicker crossed her features. Then she stood, her nose inches from Kenton's. "You're a despicable liar, Mr. McCune! There *is* no false book!"

In the next instant, the door to Kenton's room burst open and Police Chief Rennie strode into the room, ledger books in hand. *"You're* the despicable liar, Miss Hackbardt! And these prove it!" He held them inches from her face.

Clarissa gasped. Her cheeks pale as cream, she took a faltering step back, dropping onto the sofa.

Rennie passed the ledger books to Kenton, then firmly took hold of Clarissa's elbow, raising her to her feet. "Come with me, Miss Hackbardt. I'm taking you in for defrauding the Marshalls."

Suddenly energized, she twisted hard, attempting to free herself from his grip. "You can't arrest me! You promised!"

The police chief held tight, shaking his head. "Detective O'Shea and Mr. Lyons promised you immunity from prosecution for making use of embezzled money in the case with New York Central in return for your help. Defrauding the Marshalls—that's another case entirely. Now that you've produced the coin—"

"It was all Lazarus's idea to foreclose on the mortgage! Hiding the coin, falsifying the record book—"

Rennie's mouth curved in amusement. "Somehow, I knew you'd say that! Come along. You're headed for the calaboose!"

Rosalie smiled broadly as she followed them into the foyer and closed the front door behind them. When she returned to the parlor, the others were on their feet, congratulations and handshakes being exchanged all around.

O'Shea beamed. "A more cunning pair I've never seen than Ambrose and Hackbardt. Mr. Ambrose was quite the actor in civic theater back in Roch'ster, ya know."

"Small wonder he was so convincing in his new role here in Michigan," said Lyons.

"What a pity his talent went to such corrupt purposes," said Lottie.

"Same for Clarissa," said Rosalie. "I wonder if either of them will ever be redeemed."

"They'll have plenty o' time to contemplate the evil o' their ways while they're in the clink," said O'Shea.

Ben peeled off his glasses and wiped them with his handkerchief. "In the Bible, Jesus had a friend named Lazarus." Replacing his spectacles, he said, "Ambrose would see things different if he'd make Jesus *his* friend, too."

Lottie nodded. "I pray it may be so."

An idea coming to her, Rosalie turned to Kenton. "Mr. McCune, I *must* go to jail tomorrow." Following the chuckles at her inept statement, she explained. "Will you take me there, please, so I can deliver Bibles to Miss Hackbardt and Mr. Ambrose?"

"I'll take you first thing."

Several days later, however, Kenton was quite reluctant to deliver Rosalie to the depot on Park Street where she would board the train for her visit to North Carolina for Thanksgiving. The day was unusually warm and bright for November, but it didn't keep the chill from his heart when he thought about her leaving. She'd be away only six days, but they would be worrisome and lonely. While he worked in solitude at his office, he'd wonder if she was out riding with her sister and Willy Jo. While he ate Thanksgiving dinner with Ben, Lottie, and the Doyle sisters, he'd imagine Rosalie seated across from her longtime friend, steeped in reminiscences of their childhood.

Pulling to a halt in front of the depot, he tried to put away such thoughts and cherish these last few minutes with the young lady he was lifting from his surrey. Her brown braid hat trimmed with silk ribbons and velvet flowers, her matching cloak with its ruffled collar, seemed to accent the brown in her eyes and emphasize the pure ivory of her complexion. Her image would remain keen in his mind for a long time to come. He could only pray that she would return in a few days, as she had promised, to help her aunt and uncle with their confectionery—now renamed the Queen City Candy Shoppe— during the busy Christmas season.

His hands remained at her waist a few moments longer than necessary when setting her on the boardwalk in front of the depot. As he gazed into her brown eyes, she offered a modest smile.

"I'm looking forward to returning north for the winter. You'd better have cold weather and snow waiting for me when I come back!"

He managed a twitch of a smile. "I'll order some up for you."

Arranging transfer of her trunk, he picked up her small valise, offering his free arm to escort her to the platform where she would board. Her train approached, and its destinations were announced.

She turned to him, her eyes sparkling. "Come to North Carolina for Thanksgiving!"

"I . . ."

"Go home, pack your bags, and take the next train south. Mama would welcome you with open arms, and you know it!"

"Rosalie, please," he said without conviction.

"Don't you want to spend Thanksgiving with me?"

"You know I do."

"Then come!"

CHAPTER 18

North Carolina

Rosalie's heart fluttered as she opened the door to welcome the Winthrops to their traditional day-after-Thanksgiving pot-luck buffet. After a holiday filled with Foxe family aunts, uncles, and cousins, and a feast that produced leftovers too abundant and delicious to be fed to the hogs, the neighborly get-together had become a yearly, less formal luncheon she had cherished from childhood.

But this year, it held special meaning. It would be the first time she'd seen Willy Jo since she'd left for Michigan at the start of the summer. How much easier the reunion would have been with Kenton at her side, but he had remained in Traverse City after all. Now, she watched closely as Willy Jo came up the walk behind Bobby Dan and his mother. Mr. Winthrop's hand rested lightly on his elder son's shoulder, then he leaned close, saying something meant only for Willy Jo's ear that brought a smile to both their faces. She couldn't recall when she'd seen the two of them so at ease with one another.

Then Willy Jo's gaze met hers. She offered a tentative smile. He returned an equally uncertain one. The awkward moment passed when his mother entered the foyer.

Mrs. Winthrop took Rosalie's hands in hers. "Welcome home, honey! It's so good to see you. You look wonderful!" She brushed a kiss against Rosalie's cheek, bringing an aura of rose perfume with it.

Rosalie returned the affection. "And you, Mrs. Winthrop."

Bobby Dan followed his mother inside. His impish grin firmly in place, he reached into his jacket. "I've brought you a little present!" Out popped a huge bouquet of silk flowers.

Rosalie laughed. "I can see you're as tricky as you ever were, Bobby Dan."

Mr. Winthrop entered on his younger son's heels. "Trickier, if that's possible. Hello, Rosalie. You're lookin' well."

"Likewise, Mr. Winthrop."

He passed through the foyer, leaving her alone to face Willy Jo. He gazed into her eyes, his familiar blue ones reflecting the nervous anticipation she felt within. Undercurrents of conversation drifted from the parlor as Vanda Mae and her folks welcomed Willy Jo's family, but for the moment, Rosalie stood tongue-tied.

On past holidays, long separations at school had prompted prolific conversation. But not today. They were students no longer, and the distance between them was beginning to resemble the Yadkin, wide and silent.

But even the Yadkin was bridgeable, and when Rosalie finally found the right words, they erupted in spurts, nearly colliding with Willy Jo's.

"You're looking well."

"You're looking fine."

"It's nice to be home." She nibbled the inside of her lip. Her sentiment was only true in part.

"Good to have you back." He shifted his weight, and she wondered if his regard for her had shifted as well.

Feeling as if an eternity has lapsed in only a few awkward moments, she gestured toward the parlor. "Let's join the others. The buffet will be ready soon."

In the parlor, though Willy Jo took the chair beside hers, his focus turned to Vanda Mae, who was sitting on the couch next to his brother. While Bobby Dan performed a card trick, eliciting amazement and lively applause from everyone else, Willy Jo remained subdued.

Later, at the dining table, he was equally restrained when Vanda Mae drew stories from Bobby Dan about his experiences as an itinerant performer. But when Mr. Winthrop took up the subject of hog farming, Willy Jo shared his opinion willingly and confidently. As his daddy listened attentively, Rosalie thanked God that a new, healthy respect had been flourishing between them since their reconciliation.

As the meal neared an end, the topic turned to horses. Rosalie's mother set down her fork and laid aside her napkin. "I know of at least four horses in the meadow that would love some exercise on the trail through the woods, and I think you young folks ought to take it upon yourselves to grant their wish."

Vanda Mae was the first to respond. "I can't think of a better way to spend the afternoon! If I may be excused—"

Mama waved her off. "Go! All of you! And leave us older folks to our parlor games."

~~~

Rosalie and Vanda Mae changed into suitable riding attire while Willy Jo and Bobby Dan helped Gaspar bring the horses into the stable and saddle them. When Rosalie and Vanda Mae joined them, Rosalie suggested the route. "Let's ride down by the river. It's been nearly half a year since I've seen it."

Bobby Dan chuckled. "Same for me. We ought to check and see if it's still there."

Vanda Mae laughed. "If not, you ought to add that to your repertoire of magic tricks—making a river change its course!"

He pulled a wry smile. "Come on, I'll give you a hand up." They were on their horses and gone in an instant.

Willy Jo patiently helped Rosalie mount Daddy's trusty sorrel. When they came to the gate at the opposite side of the meadow, he dismounted to open it for her.

She quickly passed through, telling him, "You take the lead, Willy Jo. You know the river paths far better than I."

As they walked their horses into the woods, Rosalie made small talk about her aunt and uncle in Michigan, but it was obvious Willy Jo was barely listening. Minutes later, when they entered an opening on the bank of the Yadkin, she said, "Willy Jo, I'd like to stop for a spell by the river."

Without a word, he dismounted and helped her down.

She watched the water laze its way downstream, tasted the sweet tanginess of a muscadine that had dried on its vine, and listened to the echoing voices of Vanda Mae and Bobby Dan as they shouted nonsense across the water. With a silent prayer that the Lord would give her the right words to say, she turned to face Willy Jo.

Despite his solemn expression, she made an attempt at a smile. "Things surely are different than I remember."

Looking past her to the watery scene, he shrugged. "The river seems the same to me, except maybe the reflection of the trees now that fall's come."

She drew a breath and spoke quietly. "I wasn't referring to the river, Willy Jo, I was referring to us." Her words capturing his full attention, she continued. "We were the same for so many years, the best of friends." Looking deep into his eyes, she added, "Though neither of us ever admitted it, we had assumptions about the future, assumptions that we'd always be together."

She hadn't meant to sound quite so melancholy. Her words caused an uneasy twitch beneath his left eye.

He drew a tight breath as if to speak, but remained silent.

She continued, adjusting her tone to sound lighter. "Like I said, things are different now. We've gone in separate directions. Other people and places have become important, where they weren't before." Though she stood only inches from Willy Jo, and was still gazing into his eyes, it was Kenton's face she longed to see, and Kenton's touch she longed to feel when the young man she'd known from childhood reached for her hand.

Reading the apprehension in his countenance, Rosalie spoke on. "In the time we've been apart, I can see you've grown fond of Vanda Mae. I can't think of anyone I'd rather have sweet on my sister than you, Willy Jo."

His brow lifted. "You knew?"

She smiled, giving his hand a squeeze. "It's more obvious than you think."

Breaking off contact, he propped his foot on a stump and leaned his elbow on his knee. Chin in hand, he regarded her thoughtfully. "You're sweet on a gentleman up North."

Though she'd contemplated this moment for days, her heart paused. "Yes, Willy Jo, I am."

He gave a quick nod. "Michigan agrees with you. When are you going back?" Color rushed to his cheeks. "I . . . I didn't mean that the way it sounded."

She chuckled. "Sending me packing already, are you?"

He hung his head.

She lifted his chin with her gloved finger. "No need for embarrassment. I'm leaving the day after tomorrow. I'll be spending Christmas there." The thought, *and maybe the rest of my life,* came to mind, but she left the sentiment unspoken. Hearing Vanda Mae and Bobby Dan approaching on the trail, she said, "It's time you and I swap riding partners. You ride back with Vanda Mae. I'll go with your brother."

As she followed Bobby Dan back to the stable, her heart longed to board the train for the ride north.

CHAPTER 19

A month later, the jangle of sleigh bells, the muted thuds of Judge's hooves against the snow-covered street, the frosting overhanging the rooftop and tapering to long, narrow fingers of ice at the corners made Rosalie's world full of wonder as Kenton turned into the driveway following the midnight Christmas Eve service at St. Francis Church.

In the front parlor window, the spruce tree they had decorated hours earlier now stood as a dark sentinel, its candles snuffed. Lottie and Ben had retired some time ago, exhausted from their efforts to keep up with demand for Christmas candy so popular they could hardly believe their own success. Rosalie, too, felt the fatigue of long hours in the confectionery during the weeks since Thanksgiving.

Using unique molds her aunt and uncle had recently purchased, she had helped them turn out scores of red and yellow hard candy novelties in a vast array of shapes. Santa in a sleigh pulled by reindeer, a frog on a bicycle, a woman riding a horse sidesaddle, a dog begging, a fox holding a goose and an eagle, a large ship, a multi-car train, and dozens of smaller candy figures the likes of angels and snowmen had disappeared from the shelves almost as quickly as they had cooled. Twelve-, fourteen-, even sixteen-hour days had been commonly spent cooking, pouring, and trimming the delectable treats. The efforts had taken their toll, but the thrill of Rosalie's first winter in the North coupled with the excitement of the long-awaited holiday now arriving, kept drowsiness at bay.

Kenton parked by the side door, folded back the bearskin robe that had been keeping them warm, and helped her down, promising, "I'll be in as soon as I unhitch Judge."

"I'll put on some hot chocolate." She hurried inside. Though the warmth of the kitchen offered relief from the nippy temperatures, she wasn't at all put off by the frigid Northern Michigan winter as some had predicted. Measuring cocoa, sugar, and milk into a pan and lighting the gas burner, she chuckled to herself recalling the dire predictions of the well-meaning Doyle sisters who had prophesied her hasty retreat to North Carolina after the first snowstorm of the season, and the equally daunting recollections sent through the mail by her very own mother who had once called Michigan her home.

But curiously, the colder the weather turned, the deeper the snow piled up, the better Rosalie liked the North. She enjoyed sleigh rides along country roads with fields so deep in white only the tops of their fence posts showed. She loved ice skating on the Reddicks' pond with Kenton's arm tight about her to keep her upright. She even loved building snowmen and tossing snowballs. Afterward, she especially appreciated the crackling fire Kenton would build in the fireplace to warm her numb fingers, ruddy cheeks, and red nose. In fact, the longer she stayed in Michigan, the longer she *wanted* to stay.

A good part of liking this place was the presence of Kenton McCune. She couldn't imagine anything that could interfere with the respect and kind regard building between them—sentiments that seemed to increase with each passing day. Kenton's affections had grown, too. She'd noticed it in the way he would squeeze her hand or kiss her cheek for the most trivial of reasons—moments she treasured in her heart.

He'd been especially considerate of her with Christmas approaching, asking time and again if she was sure she wanted to remain in Traverse City rather than returning to North Carolina for the holiday celebration with her kin. Though she'd suffered mild longings to visit Home Church with her family for the Moravian Christmas Eve service, those desires quickly died away when plans arose to attend the midnight celebration at St. Francis.

At the sound of Kenton stamping the snow off his boots on the porch, she took mugs down from the shelf and poured the cocoa. She was rummaging in the cupboard for the tin of marshmallows Aunt Lottie had made last night when he stepped up behind her, his hands encircling her waist.

He turned her toward him, a subtle smile tugging his carefully trimmed mustache and goatee upward, softening the strong angles that defined his cheeks and jaw.

~~~

"Merry Christmas, Miss Foxe." When he bent to kiss her cheek, the essence of her peach toilet water temporarily displaced the aroma of hot chocolate. And when her brown eyes met his, their warmth hinted at the unspoken kinship between them.

"Merry Christmas, Mr. McCune." Her words, expressed in a disappearing southern drawl, were quiet and breathy, making him wish more than ever that this time, she would return his kiss with one of her own, but he knew better than to expect it, even though this *was* Christmas.

Quelling the temptation to kiss her on the lips, he said, "I see you have the chocolate ready."

"All but the marshmallows. They're here somewhere." She released herself to continue her search.

"I'll rekindle the fire while you look for them."

In the parlor fireplace, the logs he'd started earlier for Ben and Lottie had died to a few red coals. Nurturing them to flame with the help of crumpled newspaper and kindling, he laid on a maple log and began moving the furniture. Customarily, he and Rosalie sat facing each other in the winged chairs on either side of the fireplace, the low mahogany table centered between them. Tonight, he had a new arrangement in mind. Moving chairs and table aside, he set the love seat in front of the fireplace and confiscated the knitted throw from the back of the sofa. He was checking his jacket pocket for the tiny box he'd stashed there earlier when Rosalie entered the room carrying a tray of cocoa and Christmas cookies.

She paused, studying the new arrangement. He took the tray from her, set it on the table, then led her to the center of the love seat, draping her with the throw and serving her a mug and cookie before settling on the floor at her feet.

The crackling of the fire seemed to suffice for conversation while they sipped their hot cocoa. Munching one of Rosalie's angel-shaped sugar cookies, Kenton privately reviewed the words he wanted to say.

A few days after Rosalie's return from North Carolina last month he had decided that tonight was the night he'd ask for her hand in marriage, but now that the time had come, the significance of the occasion seemed to grow more daunting with each passing minute. Doubts that had seemed of little moment, now loomed large.

Perhaps she was too young. More than ten years separated them in age. Though she seemed to genuinely enjoy his company, and a wonderful companionship had flourished between them in the past several months, perhaps she wasn't ready for a lifetime commitment.

His fear of rejection heightened at the thought that, despite claims of no future plans with Willy Jo, the lad had been her neighbor and close friend for as long as she could remember. The possibility existed that they would find their way back to each other if only Kenton wouldn't come between.

No sooner had he discarded that notion, than another one popped up to take its place. He'd never met Rosalie's father. Maybe he should wait until he'd seen the man in person. Though he'd secretly written her folks three weeks ago asking permission for their daughter's hand in marriage, and their blessings had been given posthaste, Rosalie might prefer that he visit her childhood home himself before agreeing to take him as her partner for life.

He wondered, too, if the novelty of snow and cold weather would wear thin once the excitement of the holidays had passed. She appeared to be enjoying herself immensely on their wintertime outings, but the cold season had only begun. She could very well tire of it and go packing for a warmer climate before spring came knocking on Michigan's door.

The very thought brought another dreaded possibility to mind. He recalled the day Ben and Lottie learned their mortgage was in default and he had gone to the train depot to intervene with Rosalie on their behalf. If they were married, would she run home to Tanglewood at the first sign of trouble?

He couldn't possibly know the answer. Nor could he be absolutely certain that, despite all outward signs, she cared enough for him to accept a proposal of marriage, but he was more than certain of this—over time, he'd grown to love this Southern belle. She was on his mind morning, noon, night, and in his dreams. She'd given new meaning to his work and his leisure. He'd begun including her in every thought, every plan, every decision. And he couldn't imagine his future without her. For his own sake, for his own peace of mind, he must discover whether her sentiments for him ran as deeply as his for her.

He had eaten his way through two more of Rosalie's angel cookies when he set his mug aside and turned to face her on one knee. Her features, bathed in the soft glow of firelight, alluded to a peace and happiness within, but her lovely countenance couldn't completely quell the quiver inside him.

~~~

Kenton's hands trembled when he gently grasped Rosalie's. His expression was solemn, too. And the way he was kneeling at her side could mean only one thing.

She had sensed this moment building. She had dreamed, wished—even prayed for it to come. And she had hoped that it might arrive this very evening.

Now that it appeared her dreams and wishes were about to come true, her blood rushed. The notion of a lifetime with one man was almost too much to comprehend. Maybe she wouldn't be a good wife. Maybe someone better suited to Kenton, someone from the North, would come along if she would only go back to her Carolina home.

But how could she? Beyond any measure of emotion she'd experienced in her life, she had grown to love Kenton McCune. Being with him made her happy. Being parted from him made her miserable.

Her ponderings faded away as he began to speak.

"Miss Foxe," he paused to look directly into her eyes. His soft gaze, so full of tenderness, melted her heart.

"Yes, Mr. McCune?"

Silence stretched on. She'd never seen him at a loss for words. Somehow, she must ease his tension.

"Mr. McCune, I'd be honored if you'd call me by my Christian name. I believe we are sufficiently familiar with one another to dispense with more formal address."

He nodded. "Rosalie . . ."

The sound of her name, caressed by Kenton's tongue, was more captivating than any her ear had heard.

"I know we've run in separate channels for most of our lives. But of late, God has granted us the grace to draw nearer and nearer. And now . . ." His mouth tilted upward. "Now, my life is completely, divinely, gloriously lost in yours, and I can think of only one remedy for it." Squeezing her hands, he continued.

"Rosalie, will you be my wife?"

Her heart stopped and then fluttered wildly. She flung her arms about his neck and pressed her cheek tight against his.

"Yes, Kenton! Yes! A hundred times, yes!"

CHAPTER 20

A week later, on the way to Reddicks' for New Year's Eve, Rosalie kept her hands snug inside her new rabbit fur muff, mindful of the soreness in her throat and the occasional chill running up her spine that portended the onset of a cold. She suffered a pang of guilt knowing she might infect others, but the Reddicks had a tradition of bringing in the New Year with Kenton, and Susan's heart was set on making this night a special celebration of his betrothal as well. So Rosalie kept her discomfort a secret, privately promising herself she'd rest once the holiday was over.

Inside her muff, she couldn't keep her hands still, twisting her new ring around her left, fourth finger. Putting worries of illness out of mind, she turned her thoughts to the large center stone and each of the smaller ones on either side, and mentally pictured the custom design Kenton had requested from the jeweler, J.N. Martinek—white diamonds banded in platinum, their mounts surrounded by a delicate filigree of yellow gold. Though she'd worn it for a week, she was still fascinated by the feel of it. And her heart soared each time she pondered the fact that in the months to come, on a date not yet determined, she would take Kenton McCune's name for her own.

~~~

Kenton stole a glance at his betrothed and smiled to himself. He couldn't remember when he'd felt as lighthearted and full of joy as he had this past week, knowing Rosalie's affections for him were as ardent as his for her.

A minute later, he turned down Reddicks' drive. Puddles of water stood on the hard pack of snow and ice, testimony to the unseasonably warm temperatures that had blown in on gusty breezes two days ago, melting most of the snow. He eased Judge ahead, cautious of the slick conditions made slipperier by the standing water. In the distance, he heard a faint rumble.

"Is that thunder?" Rosalie asked.

He nodded.

"Do you think it will actually rain?"

"It might."

"I suppose the last of my beautiful snow is going to melt away, and the ice on the skating pond will go soft."

He chuckled. "Don't fret. Winter's just begun. You'll see plenty more snow and ice before the spring thaw." Pulling to a halt by Reddicks' front door, he helped her down from the buggy, wrapping his arm tightly about her waist to guide her along the wet walkway to the front porch.

The wreathed door opened within moments of his knock. He'd last seen John and Susan at church on Christmas Eve, and had been mighty surprised they'd come, knowing John hadn't darkened the door of a church since the death of his wife. Now, both father and daughter welcomed him and Rosalie with smiles, and Kenton couldn't remember ever seeing such peacefulness in John's countenance.

Their exchange of New Year's greetings in the foyer was interrupted by the patter of rain against the tin roof.

Helping Rosalie off with her coat, Kenton said, "I'd better put my rig in the stable before it gets soaked."

To Susan, John said, "Why don't you and Miss Foxe set the fixin's out on the buffet. We'll be right in."

Alone with John in the stable, Kenton commented as he wrapped Judge's reins about a post. "There's something different about you, John. You're looking better than you have in a long time—more rested." Had the change resulted from John's recent visit to church?

John winked, a new light shining from his blue eyes. "I *feel* better. I'll explain sometime. Right now, our ladies are waitin'." He put a feed bag on Judge and headed for the door.

~~~

Inside, Rosalie had accepted Susan's profuse compliments on her ring, exchanged excited hugs over her betrothal, and had helped her set the buffet with a wassail bowl, cups, and a tray of holiday sweets by the time the men returned. After much prodding from Susan, Rosalie let Kenton catch her under the mistletoe the young girl had hung especially for their benefit in the doorway between parlor and dining room, although she worried that he, too, would soon suffer from a sore throat. Afterward, while sitting beside him on the love seat, chills plagued her, despite the warmth of conversation being shared. And in spite of the delectable flavor of the young girl's gingerbread cookies, miniature taffy tarts, and wassail, she would have preferred a cup of hot chicken bouillon to soothe her worsening throat and ease her recurring chills.

At least the game they played to occupy the hours till midnight required little talking. While the pitter-patter of rain gave way to the silence of a winter eve's snowfall, she took turns with the others acting out various words and phrases in a contest of charades. At the stroke of twelve, when John lit into a lively chorus of *Auld Lang Syne,* she was thankful the others didn't notice she was barely singing.

Pulling on his coat, Kenton told Rosalie, "I'll bring the buggy around. We'd better go before the snow gets any thicker."

While Kenton headed to the stable with John, Rosalie and Susan cleared the buffet and washed dirty cups and plates. Kenton was escorting her down the wet walkway of snow-covered ice when a chilling wind whipped against her, plastering her with huge, wet snowflakes coming so thick and fast, even John, standing by the carriage only a few feet away, was momentarily obscured from view.

He held Judge steady as Kenton helped her aboard. "The weather's turnin' bad in a hurry. Why don't the two of you stay the night?"

Kenton shook his head. "We'd better get home while we can. Thanks, anyway."

He climbed aboard and urged Judge ahead. At the gelding's reluctance to move, he slapped the reins gently against his back. "Get along, Judge! We're going home!"

With uncertain steps, he started down the driveway.

Low spots that had been overflowing with water from rain and melting snow were now beginning to crust over with ice. Kenton scolded Judge many times to get him through the crunchy puddles. Several minutes later, he finally turned onto the main roadway.

The flickering flames of the buggy's brass lanterns revealed little of the country road on such a black night, but reflections against the fresh blanket of white revealed that the deep drainage ditch had filled with runoff, and several patches of ice lay exposed by drifting snow. Rosalie was wondering how Kenton could see far enough ahead to know the way when a cottontail rabbit scampered across the road only few feet in front of Judge.

The gelding shied, then slipped.

The carriage jostled and jerked.

"Easy, boy! Easy!" Kenton commanded.

Veering left, then right, Judge danced sideways, slipped again, and went down on his chest and belly. Frantic, he overturned the buggy on its right side and slid helplessly off the road dragging the rig with him into the flooded ditch.

Kenton pressed like a dead weight against Rosalie. She screamed, the sound ripping from her sore throat amidst the horrifying shrieks of a horse in intense pain, and Kenton's futile commands.

The icy waters of the ditch quickly seeped into the rig, soaking the lap robe and her woolen overcoat. Somehow, Kenton managed to climb out and pull her out the left side. Standing thigh-deep in frigid water, she clutched tightly to Kenton's hand as he began climbing out of the ditch to the road. Losing her foothold on the icy incline, then her grip, she fell backward into the ditch with a splash.

"Rosalie!" Kenton tromped into the water to pick her up.

On her feet again, teeth chattering, she said, "I'm not hurt, just cold and wet."

Kenton clasped her tightly to his side, half-dragging her up the incline to the snowy road. Giant, wet snowflakes were falling in waves so thick, she could barely see Judge still struggling a few feet away, but she could clearly hear his wailing neighs.

Once on level ground, though quaking with a severe chill, she told Kenton, "You've got to help Judge!"

"Stay here. I'll be right back!"

As she stood shivering, the wind howled, plastering thick snow against her dark wrap, giving her an overcoat of white. As she shook off the frosty adornment, she could hear Kenton splashing into the flooded ditch again, then talking to Judge, telling him he'd come back soon and get him out.

Returning to her side moments later, he wrapped his arm tight about her and started up the road toward Reddicks'.

"I've got to get you inside where you can warm up and dry off. Then I've got to get back here with a rifle as quick as I can. Judge's leg is broken. There's no saving him."

"I'm so . . . sorry." She replied between uncontrollable spasms of chattering teeth.

Pausing to gaze at her, he kissed her wet cheek and hugged her to him. "Thank God you're only wet, not hurt." Clutching her against his side, he started toward Reddick's again.

"I should have listened to John! I shouldn't have forced Judge!"

"You did what you thought was best," Rosalie argued sympathetically.

"And look where it got us!" he replied with disgust. "When we get back to the house, I want you to get out of those wet clothes, change into something dry, and stay by the fire while John and I see to Judge."

"But . . . you're wet, too!"

"I'll be all right."

Realizing further discussion was futile, and with her chattering teeth and sore throat, nigh unto impossible, Rosalie kept her silence and concentrated on the challenge of keeping her feet beneath her on the trek up the long, slippery driveway.

The Reddick home was dark as a tomb when they reached the front door. Finding it unlocked, Kenton helped Rosalie inside and announced their presence. Soon, both John and Susan, donned in long flannel gowns and sleeping caps, came hurrying down the stairs by the light of an oil lamp. Within minutes, Susan had the kitchen stove roaring with fire, the tea kettle filled, and after phoning Ben and Lottie, Kenton had gone with John to see about Judge.

As Rosalie divested herself of her waterlogged clothing, Susan hung it near the stove to dry, then wrapped her in a thick, woolen blanket and set her in a rocking chair close to the stove. "You stay right there and warm up while I find a gown for you." She headed upstairs.

Rosalie continued to shudder with chills. In addition to the soreness in her throat, she now had a headache, and pain in her legs and back which she attributed to the accident.

The clock in the parlor was striking half past one when Susan returned with a pink flannel gown. "This used to be Mama's, but you can use it." She held it near the stove to warm it before handing it to Rosalie.

"Are you sure?" Rosalie hardly recognized her own voice, weak and thin.

"You sound terrible."

Rosalie sighed. "I'm coming down with a cold. Better keep your distance. I don't want you to catch it."

"I'll make you some tea and honey. It ought to soothe your throat."

Susan took a china teapot from the shelf, warmed it with a small amount of boiling water from the kettle on the stove, then added several spoonsful of tea leaves before filling it to the top and covering it with a cozy.

By the time the clock struck two, Rosalie had sipped a full cup of strong tea sweetened with a generous portion of honey, but was feeling no improvement. Aside from her own discomfort, she worried about Kenton, fearing he'd taken a bad chill and would be seriously ill.

Susan pulled a second rocker near the stove, and fell sound asleep beneath a blanket, unmindful that her fire was beginning to die out.

Suffering constant chills, Rosalie hated to stir from her own woolen cocoon to add wood, but neither was she about to needlessly waken the girl. Reluctantly unwrapping herself, she opened the fire box, tossed in two sticks of hardwood, and latched the door as quietly as possible.

Susan stirred and yawned, but didn't wake. Rosalie envied her the ability to sleep, being too beset by her own discomforts to stay in slumber land for more than an hour at a stretch. When she awoke at three, she felt feverish, and knew *this* cold was going to be worse than others she'd had. She stoked the fire and settled down in her rocker again, increasingly concerned for the welfare of Kenton and John.

An hour later, Rosalie awoke with tightness in her chest. She again added wood to the stove, then scraped frost from the window overlooking the stable and peered out. Light spilled onto white drifts of snow creeping higher and higher by the stable door, but neither Kenton nor John was in view.

She retreated to her rocker, waking at five with a hacking cough and feeling as though someone had slipped a band of steel about her lungs, making every breath painful. She retrieved her handkerchief from the pocket of her dress, still drying by the stove, so she could stifle her coughing fits, then snuggled into her rocker again. Her misery continued, as well as her worry for the men, until they finally came through the kitchen door a half hour later.

CHAPTER 21

Kenton knew the moment he heard Rosalie's cough and saw the blue tinge to her skin that, despite the smile with which she greeted him, she was suffering from more than a cold. And when he pressed his lips to her forehead, he worried about her high fever, as well.

Her brown eyes, rimmed with fatigue, met his. "Are you all right?" Her voice barely broke a whisper. "I've worried every minute that you'd catch your death out there." She lapsed into a fit of coughing.

He touched the back of his hand to her burning cheek. "I'll be just fine. Don't try to talk anymore."

She nodded.

He returned to the side entry and hung up his coat.

John kissed Susan's cheek. She stirred, mumbled acknowledgment of his presence, and fell asleep again even before her father had removed his jacket, hat, and gloves. Emerging from the side entry with Kenton, John said, "If you come upstairs a minute, I'll find you a change of clothes. They'll hang a little loose on you, but it's better than stayin' in wet ones."

Thankful for John's offer, Kenton followed his friend into the second floor bedroom. Removing his sodden pants, shirt, and underthings, he said, "I'm worried about Rosalie. She's running a high fever, and that cough is no simple cold. I'd like to set up a cot by the kitchen stove and ring up Dr. Sawyer."

"We can do better than that. We'll haul down the bed in the spare room." His brows narrowing, John added, "I don't think the doc will be able to make it out here from town, though, the way the road's driftin', but maybe he can tell us what to do."

Within minutes, they had erected a single bed in the kitchen, and with Susan's help, made it up with fresh sheets, layered it with woolen blankets, and tucked Rosalie snugly in. Whether Dr. Sawyer could make a house call or not was of little matter, for when Kenton picked up the phone to ring him, the line was dead. Placing the instrument on its hook with a firm click, he tried to think what to do for Rosalie.

Susan spoke up. "Mama kept a medical book upstairs. I'll go fetch it."

Though Kenton didn't speak of it in front of Rosalie, he suspected she had contracted pneumonia, and when he sat down to the kitchen table with a lamp and read the symptoms described in the medical book, he discovered his fears were well-founded. Studying the treatments for such a case, he took John aside, speaking confidentially. "I'm fairly certain Rosalie has pneumonia. Quinine is recommended, and a mustard poultice. Do you—"

Even before he could finish asking, John had gone to retrieve a bottle of quinine from the top shelf of a kitchen cupboard, and ground mustard from the pantry. While Kenton administered a full dose of the tonic, Susan fetched several old pieces of cotton from a rag bag and set about mixing the mustard with the beaten white of an egg and a small amount of flour. She spread the paste on one of the cloths, folded it over, and layered other cloths on top of it to prevent soiling her mother's nightgown.

While Susan applied the poultice to Rosalie's chest, Kenton and John retreated to the dining room. Too preoccupied to sit at the table with his friend, Kenton leaned against the sideboard and stared idly down at the turned-up cuffs of the overly long pants John had loaned him. The sound of Rosalie's tight, frequent cough worried Kenton too much to care that the flannel pant legs didn't quite match in length. A heavy gust of wind battered the clapboard siding, making it creak, drawing John out of his chair and eliciting comment.

"This storm's gonna blow awhile, from the sounds of it."

His words only heightened Kenton's frustration. "Let it blow. When daylight comes, I'm going after a doctor. You'll loan me Penny, won't you?"

John shook his head.

"Then I'll go on foot. I've got to get Rosalie proper medical attention."

John lay his hand on Kenton's shoulder. "It was bad enough out there draggin' Judge back to the barnyard and towin' your buggy to the stable. We nearly froze our faces off before we got the job done, and it's a lot worse now."

His jaw taut, Kenton said, "It's my fault Rosalie's sick. I won't be to blame for her not getting proper care."

John's hand tightened, sending pain into Kenton's shoulder. "And I won't be to blame for lettin' my best friend commit suicide. You're stayin' inside this house if I have to strap you to a kitchen chair with ten yards of barbed wire!"

Kenton made no reply. A moment later, evidently interpreting silence as acquiescence, John released him, but inside, Kenton was seething. He sat in the empty rocker beside Susan, realizing he couldn't possibly stay there the whole day long listening to Rosalie's labored breathing and watching the young woman he loved get worse with each passing hour. If John wouldn't loan him Penny, he'd head out to the privy, sneak to the stable, then take the mare and go for help.

But by daybreak, snow had drifted so thickly against the side door, Kenton and John together could barely get it open, and before John could shovel a path to the outhouse and stable, he had to attach a length of rope to his waist to make certain he could find the house again, for the air was too thick with snow to see the outbuildings.

With a heavy heart, Kenton returned to the rocker beside Rosalie's bed. Susan dozed in the chair next to his, then went upstairs to her own bed, telling him to call her if Rosalie needed her. He rested his head against the chair back, drifting into fitful naps that alternated between moments of wakefulness and worry over Rosalie's coughing, and awareness of John tossing wood into the kitchen stove and warming himself there before returning to the cold outdoors.

By mid-morning, with Susan still upstairs asleep and John outdoors, Kenton was too fidgety to remain still. He filled a wash basin with cool water, dipped a clean rag in it, and sat on the edge of Rosalie's bed, sponging off her face and neck, pushing up the sleeves of her nightgown to wipe down her arms, meeting no resistance even when he ministered to her crippled right one. As he worked over her, he noticed certain changes from hours earlier. She was perspiring now, her forehead felt cooler to the touch, and her cough, though not eliminated, was less severe—reactions detailed in the medical text that could result from a full dose of quinine, and could mean the disease had been aborted in its early stages. He silently thanked God that the attack of pneumonia had been so quickly thwarted.

Setting wash basin aside, he took Rosalie's hand in his. "Would you like some tea or broth? You should try to take something."

"Broth."

"Crackers?"

She nodded.

Kenton searched the kitchen cupboards, ice box, and pantry, coming up with turkey broth left from the Christmas bird, a pan to heat it in, a tin of soda crackers, and even a small tray to serve it on. He poured a mug of the broth for himself as well, and sat in the rocker sipping the soothing liquid as Rosalie drank hers. They were finishing their last swallows when John came inside, his cheeks and nose bright red.

Divesting himself of jacket, cap, and gloves, he stood between Rosalie's bed and the stove, warming his hands as he cast a backward glance at the patient. "You're feelin' better, I see."

"I am." Rosalie replied, her cough aggravated by even those two tiny words.

As Kenton set their dirty dishes in the wash basin, he stated cheerfully, "She'll be good as new in a couple of days."

John made no reply. Done warming his hands, he stoked the stove, set coffee on to boil, then opened the ice box and hauled out a bowl of eggs, slab of bacon, and pitcher of milk. "Anyone for scrambled eggs and bacon?"

Rosalie shook her head, mouthing the words, "No, thank you."

Feeling relieved at her turn for the better, Kenton said, "Eggs and bacon would hit the spot with me. Can I help?"

While tending the stove, John talked Kenton through instructions for setting the table. The aroma of fried bacon must have aroused Susan's appetite. Soon, she was downstairs adding a place setting to the dining table and a bowl of the oranges she'd found in her stocking on Christmas morning.

When Kenton had helped himself to a portion of the fluffy eggs and three strips of crisp bacon, he told Susan and John, "If only the weather would improve as quickly as Rosalie, we could go home."

His voice low, John replied, "Her turn for the better could be a temporary thing."

Irked, Kenton stated quietly but confidently, "She'll be on her feet in no time. Mark my words."

With lines cutting deep into his forehead, John said, "I hope you're right."

The day passed in two more cycles of hopefulness followed by worry. Each dose of quinine produced improvements. When Rosalie was feeling relief, Kenton would venture from the house to help John with the shoveling, and the chores in the stable.

When the medicine was wearing off and Rosalie was beset by a return of the coughing, fever, and labored breathing, Kenton would remain by her side, laden with guilt over the accident that had brought on her illness. He asked himself time and again why he hadn't listened to John and agreed to stay overnight in the first place. Pangs of guilt set off prayers for her recovery, and prayers, too, that this first day of 1901 was no indication that a year of troubles would follow.

He sat with Rosalie throughout the night, half-awake most of the time. The second day of the New Year passed much the same as the first. Rosalie's condition seemed no worse, but no better, and neither did the weather. Again, Kenton stayed with her through the night, praying that God would bring her lasting relief with every wheezing breath she took, and asking himself just as often how he could live with himself if she should fail to recover.

The relief God granted on the third day of January, however, concerned neither Rosalie, nor his worry and guilt, but the world outside the Reddick home, described succinctly by John at six in the morning when he opened the door to go to the stable.

Holding his lantern high, he reported, "No wind. It's stopped snowing. I'm goin' to clear the driveway soon as I tend the horses." He closed the door with a thud, leaving the kitchen in darkness again.

Rosalie stirred, mumbled something, then coughed several times into her handkerchief.

Kenton lit an oil lamp to administer her morning medicine, immediately alarmed by the revelations of the flickering flame. The beauty of Rosalie's oval face was masked by anxiety and distress that hadn't been there the day before. Her white handkerchief was badly stained by rusty sputa from her coughing spells. Touching the back of his hand to her forehead, he realized she was burning up though she showed no sign of perspiration.

She pushed his hand away with a feeble effort and a frail plea. "Willy Jo . . . find Shani. I need Shani."

Kenton set down the lamp, kneeling at her bedside to take both of her hands in his. "Rosalie, my love, Shani isn't here, but I'll take care of you, I promise." He kissed her hands, afraid that he couldn't keep his word, terrified of losing her, and hating himself for letting her get this way.

She started to cough and reached for her soiled handkerchief. Kenton quickly tossed it aside, substituting his own, clean one. Then he fetched the quinine, pouring the tonic into a spoon. She swallowed it with difficulty, struggling to catch her breath afterward.

He left her side long enough to pump fresh, cool water into a basin. Taking up a wet rag, he wiped her face and neck, then consulted the medical book again, searching pantry cupboards and shelves for the remedies listed for this stage of the disease. Having little success, he was about to arouse Susan when he heard her coming down the stairs. She'd no sooner stepped into the kitchen when he fired off his list of requests.

"I need carbonate of ammonia, camphor liniment, a flaxseed poultice, and lemonade with cream of tartar. Can you help me?"

"I'll try."

Listening to Rosalie suffer during the few minutes that passed while Susan gathered supplies from various parts of the house felt like a lifetime. Each labored breath, every racking cough, pierced Kenton's heart. Could any manmade decoctions could actually change the course of the disease? Prayer and home remedies were his only hope. He asked God to continue guiding him in helping the woman he desperately wanted for his wife. His hopes lifted when Susan presented him with carbonate of ammonia and camphor liniment from the kitchen cabinet, flaxseed and cream of tartar from the pantry, and all the oranges from the fruit bowl on the dining table—her substitute for lemons to make a cooling drink.

While the young girl created a syrup for the carbonate of ammonia and a poultice from the flaxseed, Kenton squeezed the oranges. Mixing in the cream of tartar, he held the glass for Rosalie to drink, administered the carbonate of ammonia, then excused himself from the room while Susan rubbed camphor liniment on Rosalie's chest, replaced her mustard poultice with the flaxseed one, and helped her to relieve herself in the chamber pot.

When Susan called him back into the room, Kenton began donning coat and boots. "If you'll stay by Rosalie awhile, I'll empty the chamber pot. Then I need to talk to your father."

"Of course." Susan took up the wet cloth to sponge off Rosalie's face.

Outdoors, the chamber pot yielded what Kenton had feared from descriptions in the medical book—scanty, high-colored urine. When he had discarded it and relieved himself in the privy, he headed to the stable, mucking out Penny's stall as he talked with John.

"Rosalie's delirious with fever. I've got to get to town and bring back the doctor."

John paused to lean on his pitchfork. "You'll never make it."

Kenton's gaze met John's. "Penny can get me there."

John sighed heavily. "There are drifts out there as high as my shoulder. The two of you will get stuck, then what are you gonna do?"

"We won't get stuck. We'll go around them. I'll take a shovel." He began untying Penny.

"Leave her be!" John warned.

Paying no heed, Kenton began backing Penny out of her stall.

John blocked his exit, shoulders back, feet apart, pitchfork erect. "We've been through this before. I won't let you risk life, limb, and *my* horse."

Kenton turned away from John's unyielding gaze. Settling his focus on Penny, he masked his anger with calm logic. "The storm's over. Rosalie's burning up. She'll die if I don't get help."

"I'll go."

Astonished by the offer, Kenton was silently asking a half-dozen questions when John began supplying answers.

"I'll clear the drive, then I'll start for town. But I won't let you leave Rosalie now. She needs you here."

Relief surged through Kenton. "I don't know how to thank you."

"Save your thanks. I might not make it. But at least I'm levelheaded enough to know when to turn back."

John put his pitchfork away and the two of them worked for an hour clearing a narrow path down the drive. Though the road was in bad shape, someone had already made tracks toward town which John could follow. In the stable once more, John went for Penny's bridle, Kenton seeing to her saddle blanket and saddle, still puzzled over John's willingness to make the difficult journey.

"I don't understand yet why you're doing this, John. What made you change your mind about going for the doctor?"

John adjusted a stirrup, then paused to answer, his expression melancholy, his words solemn. "My biggest regret is not bein' with the woman I loved when she needed me most. That's a mistake I'll live with for the rest of my life—a mistake I won't let you make."

Kenton meditated on the answer. "I'll pray you get through."

John almost smiled. "I'm countin' on it—the prayers, that is. There's only so much a man can do."

Surprised by John's new attitude, Kenton was curious to ask about the changes that had come over him, but his questions would have to wait until another time, for his friend was mounting up, heading for the stable door.

"Godspeed, John."

"Keep prayin'!"

In the house, Kenton took up his vigil at Rosalie's bedside once more. The remainder of the day passed in worry, prayer, and constant attendance to Rosalie's needs.

He sponged her face and forehead frequently, administered carbonate of ammonia in syrup every two hours, and encouraged her to sip as much orange juice as possible. When she dozed off in a fitful sleep, he tried to nap also, but he felt as if he were sleeping with one eye open, waking each time she stirred, anxious whenever she muttered Willy Jo's name in her delirium.

CHAPTER 22

As day gave way to night, so did his hopes that John would return before the morrow. Darkness settled over the countryside and in his heart, as well. He barely acknowledged Susan when she served him a hearty bowl of soup for supper. It grew cold before he'd finished more than a few spoonsful, his appetite nonexistent, and he paid little heed when she took the remains away.

He vaguely noticed when she pulled on her coat and went outdoors, assuming she'd gone to the privy. When she returned with a heavy load of firewood, he silently berated himself for neglecting chores of necessity and made an apology.

"I'm sorry, Susan. I should have done that for you. I didn't notice the wood was getting low."

She mumbled an acceptance and blew her nose. He assumed the cold air had made it run, but when she bent to stoke the stove, he caught a glimpse of her moist eyes and cheeks and realized something more serious was amiss.

"Susan, what's troubling you?"

She closed the stove door with a clank and hurried from the room.

Though reluctant to leave Rosalie's side, he could see that she was napping and tore himself away to go in search of Susan. He found her curled in a ball on the parlor sofa, quietly crying.

He lay a hand on her shoulder. "Susan, what's the matter? Tell me, please?"

She responded with racking sobs that made her entire body tremble. Looking up at him, she blubbered through her tears. "Papa's not coming back . . . he's going to die . . . Miss Rosalie's going to die . . . like Mama did!" She scrambled off the sofa and hurried toward the staircase, her uneven footsteps playing syncopation on the steps.

Kenton followed her to the bottom of the stairs. "Susan, come back! Please!"

She disappeared into the darkness of the second floor.

Drawn in two directions at once, Kenton returned to check on Rosalie. She was awake, coughing up blood, and in need of another dose of syrup. When he had administered the carbonate of ammonia and settled her down, he wondered if he should go to Susan. Anguishing over the impossibility of administering to two women at the same time, he prayed for guidance.

As if in answer to his prayer, Susan quietly slipped into the kitchen, settling on the chair beside his. Though her eyes were red, they were also dry. She wore a contrite look when she spoke. "I'm sorry I got upset. I—"

"You have every right to be. But one thing you can count on. Your father, wherever he is tonight, is safe and warm."

"I know. 'God is our refuge and strength, a very present help in trouble.'" She quoted the first verse of the forty-sixth

Psalm. "God can keep Papa safe, and He can heal Miss Rosalie, too. I just needed to ask Him, and believe."

For a moment, Kenton envied Susan's faith and the peacefulness now evident in her serene smile. He'd never seen such tranquility in the young girl, and was about to make mention of it when Rosalie stirred, mumbled his name, and coughed.

"I'm right here, my love." He rang out the washcloth and began mopping her forehead. "You're going to get over this, Rosalie. Your fever will break, and you'll feel much better."

His words were only lip service for Rosalie's benefit. In his heart, he feared she wouldn't even make it through the night, let alone the next five days described in the medical book for this stage of the disease.

When she had quieted down again, Susan told Kenton, "I'm going to make hot chocolate. Would you like some?"

He shook his head. "What I could really use is coffee. It's going to be another long night."

"I'll set some to boiling."

Later, when they had finished their hot beverages, Susan said, "I'm going up to bed. Call me if you need me."

Kenton nodded, but had no intention of interrupting the young girl's sleep. He alone was to blame for Rosalie's suffering, and he alone would tend her through the night, an endless routine of administering medicine, laying a cool, damp cloth against her forehead, and holding the small juice glass to her lips, a pattern interrupted only by moments in the privy to empty her chamber pot and relieve himself of the coffee he'd been drinking.

The following day differed little, except in mounting disappointment that John hadn't returned, and increased concern that Rosalie was growing weaker. Susan held up well, despite her father's absence, performing his chores in the stables as well as her own in the kitchen.

On the third evening of John's absence, the phone rang.

In a weak voice, John explained that though telephone service had been restored and the road was now open, both he and the doctor were suffering from a severe outbreak of influenza and incapable of travel.

Kenton immediately rang up Ben and Lottie to tell them of Rosalie's condition, learning they and several of their employees had contracted the virus and the candy factory and shop were both temporarily closed.

With a heavy heart, he returned to Rosalie's side. Somehow, she survived the next two days and nights, but the fever had sapped almost all her strength. In addition, the medicine was nearly gone. He rang the pharmacy to ask them to send out new supplies, but was told that would be impossible. Some of their own employees were sick, leaving them shorthanded, and the others were too busy with remedies and prescriptions for the sick in the city. As dusk turned to darkness on the fifth night of John's absence, Kenton stared at the tiny portion of cough suppressant that still remained and was convinced Rosalie couldn't make it through one more night.

When Susan had retired, he sat by Rosalie's side, his worry and hopelessness increasing with each passing minute. The night was measured by the rapid, shallow breaths she took and his fear that each one could be her last. At four in the morning, he administered the final dose of cough syrup. When she had settled her head against the pillow, he quietly left the kitchen. Helpless, terrified, and angry that God could let the object of his love and affection suffer so, he wandered into the parlor and slumped onto the sofa, fists tight, eyes heavenward.

"God, how can you do this?" he demanded through clenched teeth. "How can you make that innocent young woman suffer and die because of me?" Overwhelmed with grief at the thought of losing Rosalie, he cried out, "God, I hate you!"

Momentarily relieved of frustration, he forced himself to return to Rosalie and his deathwatch. Shortly after, Susan spoke to him from the dining room doorway.

"Is everything all right?"

When he turned to look at her, the gentle flickering of her candle softly illuminating her fair complexion, flowing, blond hair, and snow white robe, gave the brief impression of an angel.

He caught his breath, blinked, and looked again, this time aware of the deep concern in her eyes as she moved to the empty rocker beside his.

In a half-whisper, she spoke again. "I heard something. I thought I'd better come down and check." Her focus now on Rosalie, she reached past him to touch the back of her hand to the patient's forehead. "She's still burning up, isn't she?"

Kenton could only nod, his hope gone that Rosalie would survive more than an hour or two.

Quietly, Susan continued. "God says the prayers of faith shall save the sick."

"It's a lie," Kenton claimed in quiet anger. "I've been praying for Rosalie since she first took sick, and what good has it done?" He turned his focus on his frail beloved.

A minute passed, then Susan spoke again. "God won't forsake you. In his word, he makes that promise."

"Don't talk to me of God!" Kenton ground out. Though his gaze never left Rosalie, from the corner of his eye he saw Susan flinch. Nevertheless, he continued to vent his frustration. "The woman I love lies here struggling for every breath, and yet God stands by and watches her being strangled by disease."

"Anger won't make things better."

"How do you know? You're just a child!"

Seconds later, Susan replied with cool confidence. "I may be young, but I'm wise enough to listen to my elders. Papa told me a little while ago how sorry he is that he wasted the last couple of years being angry with God. Instead of pushing God away, he should have been seeking Him, like he is now."

Refusing to reply, Kenton busied himself sponging off Rosalie's face and neck. When he'd tossed the rag into the basin of water, Susan's hand sought his.

"'Be strong and of good courage, fear not, nor be afraid . . . for the Lord . . . will not fail thee, nor forsake thee.' Deuteronomy 31:6. Father in heaven, I claim your promises for my friends. Heal Miss Foxe of her physical ailments, and Mr. McCune of his spiritual ones. In Jesus' name, Amen." With a squeeze of his hand, she rose.

He listened to the rocking of her empty chair and the scuffing of her slippers as she parted, her prayer echoing in his mind. Beside him, Rosalie had settled into a fitful nap. He leaned his head back and closed his eyes. Horrid, nightmarish visions of Rosalie's form, lifeless and cold, barred him from sleep. He stared up at the ceiling and watched the flickering of the oil lamp play shadows against the bumps and indentations of the tin pattern. Hollow and hopeless, his mind went blank, too tired for cogent thought.

His next awareness was of a small voice.

"Kenton . . . are you awake?"

Suddenly realizing he'd fallen asleep, he sat erect, startled to discover Rosalie propped up on one elbow, staring at him.

He reached for her hand, squeezing it in his. "My darling, what is it? What can I get you?" Seeing that she was damp with perspiration, he touched the back of his hand to her forehead. She was definitely cooler than she had been a few hours earlier. Clearly, she had passed to the next stage of the disease described in the medical book as the stage of resolution. She had survived!

"I'd like a drink," she informed him. Though her voice was still weak, it was stronger than it had been in days, and even in the dim light of the oil lamp, he could see new vitality in her brown eyes.

He reached for her glass, still half full of juice, and held it to her lips. She placed her hand over his, tipping the tumbler until it was empty, then she lay back on the bed.

He set the glass aside and took up the damp rag, sponging away the beads of moisture on her forehead. The clock in the parlor chimed six.

"That feels good," she told him. "I'm better today."

Though she started coughing, the spasm was neither as severe nor prolonged as before. When she asked for the chamber pot, Kenton stepped into the parlor. Taking advantage of these private moments, he dropped to his knees beside the sofa. "Forgive me Lord. I never should have doubted you. Thank you for Rosalie's improvements, for this new day, and for every day to come, whatever happens. In Jesus' name, Amen."

In a moment of doubt, he recalled from the medical book that pneumonia could progress from one part of the lung to another, or to the other lung. Fear seized him, then lost its grip as renewed faith in God planted seeds in his heart and mind in the form of three words.

She is healed!

With solid confidence, he returned to Rosalie's side, silently praising the Lord for answering prayers, and for the wisdom and faith Susan had offered in his darkest hour

CHAPTER 23

North Carolina June 1901

Dressed in a white morning suit, Kenton stood ramrod straight in the rose-adorned gazebo specially designed by Mr. Foxe for Rosalie's garden wedding, thankful that she had insisted on a modest affair with close friends and relatives rather than giving in to the extravagant celebration Mrs. Foxe had proposed. The scent of the pink, white, and yellow blossoms enhanced by the warmth of the moist southern breeze wafted about him, accompanied by the strains of Bach's *Jesus, Joy of Man's Desiring* being played by the violin orchestra. Too nervous to look out across the rows of chairs where the last of the fifty-or-so wedding guests were being seated, he gazed past the clematis-covered fence to the meadow and frolicking horses beyond, his focus on the filly named Jewel.

The yearling, a wedding gift from Vanda Mae that had pleased both him and Rosalie in equal measure, had come with a promise from his future sister-in-law. "When she's old enough, I'll train her and deliver her to Traverse City." To Susan, who had traveled south with him and Rosalie to serve as a bridesmaid in the wedding party, Vanda Mae had said, "When you go home, you tell your daddy to save a stall for her!"

Those thoughts faded when the notes of the string ensemble gave way to the opening chords of Beethoven's *Ode to Joy* which Ben and Lottie had helped choose as the wedding march. Kenton's only regret was that they were not there to hear it. Ownership and management of both the candy factory and shop—now permanent with the recent conviction of Lazarus Ambrose—had prevented them from traveling south.

Putting regrets aside, Kenton redirected his thoughts and his attention to the processional, admiring Susan as she started down the aisle. Her limp was barely noticeable beneath the pink organdy dress that flowed about her, its modest train brushing the white runner that had been rolled out across the grass. Behind her followed Vanda Mae in a mist of yellow silk as subtle as a southern sky on a summer's morn.

Then, just as Rosalie was about to start down the aisle on the arm of her father, a carriage came racing along the driveway to rattle to a halt on the lawn at the rear of the seated guests. Anger rose within Kenton that the commotion caused by the unthinking, insensitive driver had interrupted the most poignant moment of the processional. The music stopped, guests turned to stare, and Kenton bit his tongue to keep his annoyance in check. But indignation gave way to elation the instant the newcomers emerged from the buggy.

Ben and Lottie had come after all!

With hugs for the bride, they were quickly ushered to second row seats where their beaming smiles chased away Kenton's last remnants of apprehension and anxiety.

Striking up the processional anew, violins sent stirring notes of Beethoven through the air as Rosalie approached the gazebo in a sheath of creamy satin overlaid by sheer organdy, her fair complexion veiled by a film of the same. Kenton couldn't suppress a proud grin the moment he saw her, his heart joyful when her brown eyes met his and her pretty lips parted in a beautiful smile. Then he noticed the touch of pink circling the high collar of her dress—the crimped satin bow she so frequently wore and he had as frequently admired from the first days of their acquaintance. How thoughtful that she would include it on this most special of days, and how perfectly the style of her entire wedding ensemble matched her personality. Neither frivolous nor severe, it symbolized her inner strength and her delicate beauty, qualities he most admired in the woman he had come to love more than life itself. Silently, he thanked God for rescuing her from the brink of death six months earlier and nursing her through a near-miraculous recovery that had actually made her stronger both physically and emotionally than before her illness.

As she advanced toward him to the stately rhythm of the processional, apprehension took flight, replaced by a God-given confidence that this union he was about to enter would be both fulfilling and satisfying, regardless of life's challenges.

~~~

Strains of the recessional sang out as Rosalie walked back down the aisle on her new husband's arm, the final words of the ceremony, "I now present to you Mr. and Mrs. Kenton McCune," ringing joyfully in her head.

At the rear of the rose garden, Kenton paused to press his lips to hers. When his sweet kiss ended, she opened her eyes to discover Hurricane looking on from behind the pasture fence a few feet away. The flick of his ears and bob of his head seemed to offer tacit approval.

Taking Kenton by the hand, she stepped up to the grey gelding she'd feared for years and patted his cheek. Turning to her husband, she said, "With you by my side, I believe I could even find the confidence to ride Hurricane again."

Brushing her fingertips with a kiss, Kenton smiled. "I'm sure you could, but not today. Our guests are waiting to wish us well."

~~~

Later that evening in Winston, Rosalie watched with pleasure as her husband scribed the names "Mr. and Mrs. Kenton McCune" in the register of Hotel Quincy. Tomorrow morning, they would board a train for Asheville and their honeymoon stay in the mountains, but for now, she was simply thrilled to know that the hustle and bustle of pre-wedding days had passed and within minutes she and Kenton would share none but each other's company.

Following the bell boy to their second floor accommodations, they paused in the hall while he placed their bags inside the door. Kenton dismissed him with a generous tip, then turned to her, his gaze full of love and fondness as he swept her into his arms. His sentiments were a mere whisper in her ear as he stood just outside the bridal suite.

"Mrs. Kenton McCune, all of Grand Traverse Bay couldn't hold the love I feel for you!"

With soft words of her own, she replied, "My dear and precious husband, all of the Blue Ridge Mountains couldn't hold the love I feel for you!"

His lips covering hers, he carried her across the threshold and laid her on the sumptuous mattress beneath an arched canopy dripping with white silk lace.

HISTORIC NOTES

Descriptions (but not always the exact dates) of many events in this novel were drawn from actual newspaper accounts and advertisements of 1900, including the Independence Day parade and carnival ball, Wallace Circus, and Boston Store sale in Traverse City.

Articles of note from *The Morning Record*

Friday, July 27, 1900
EVENTS IN SOCIETY

A delightful watermelon party was enjoyed on the shore of the river in front of the residence of Frank Friedrich last evening. One of the watermelons had the misfortune to fall from the basket, and it rolled into the river and was drowned, but the other served the party most pleasantly. A jolly time was enjoyed by all.

Thursday, July 19, 1900
CONDENSED NEWS OF MICHIGAN

It is announced that 15 couples from Stark County, Indiana will go to St. Joseph in a body to be married the first Sunday in August. They are members of a matrimonial club and by paying monthly assessments, sufficient funds have been collected to pay all the necessary expenses. Several hundred relatives and friends will join in the unique pilgrimage.

242

Sunday, July 22,1900
DRUNKEN SQUAW.

Called Out the Fire Department This Morning. The
entire fire department was hustled out of bed this morning at 3
o'clock by the ring of the telephone. Chief Rennie went to 210
South Division Street at the call of a lady who said that a crazy
woman had been sitting on the porch almost all night.

Rennie found a drunken squaw with a papoose. The
squaw said, "My man gone Pashabatown with one more
squaw."

She was placed in the coop, and will probably make it
hot for "her man" later.

Wednesday, July 25,1900
THE POWER OF HOME
Its Relation to Society and Its Influence In the Church

The unit of society is the home. Enrollment that
assumes to be thorough is not a registration by individuals, but
by families. If we were to say that the structure of society is
cellular, we should have to say that it is the family that
constitutes each separate cell. No man, however entire, is a
cell. No woman, however complete, is a cell. There is no
finished cell except in the grouping of several individuals
bound by the ties of domesticity. A bachelor is a dislocated
fragment. His female counterpart is in the same category. It
may not be their fault. It may lie in the necessity of their case.
Still, all in all, it is a condition foreign to divine intention.

It is to the family, therefore, that we shall have to look
as being the prime point of concern in all that relates to the
weal of our times and our kind. The strength and health of
society are to be measured by the amount of affectionate
emphasis that is laid on the home idea, and the wholesomeness
of society is simply the sanctity of the home writ large. Homes

are each of them the separate roots that carry their several contributions to the organized structure of the general life.

All of this holds whether society be considered in its religious relations, which we know as the church, or in its secular ones, known as the state. The home is the first church, and the home is the first state. There is nothing in either of the two that is not initially present in a small way inside the home circle. As regards the former there is a very important idea conserved in so arranging our church auditoriums as to combine the congregation without sacrificing the identity of its families. The pew system of worship is the deft way that our church architecture takes to teach the doctrine that each home is a little religious organism. This is one of those interesting cases where a sense of fitness, even without being distinctly conscious of it, nevertheless asserts itself and creates a very substantial expression of itself, and there is no preacher—at least there is no pastor—who does not carry distinctly in his head, and particularly in his heart, this cellular structure of his congregation and does not feel that the significance of his congregation depends not on the number of its individuals, but on the number of its families.

Rev. C.H. Parkhurst in Ladies' Home Journal.

ABOUT DONNA WINTERS

Donna adopted Michigan as her home state in 1971 when she moved there from a small town outside of Rochester, New York. She began penning novels in 1982 while working full time for an electronics company in Grand Rapids.

She resigned in 1984 following a contract offer for her first book. Since then, she has written several romance novels for various publishers, including Thomas Nelson Publishers, Zondervan Publishing House, Guideposts, and Bigwater Publishing LLC. Her nonfiction writing has been published by Chalfont House.

Her husband, Fred, an American History teacher, shares her enthusiasm for history. Together, they visit historical sites, restored villages, museums, and lake ports, purchasing books and reference materials and taking photos. She has visited Traverse City and walked the historic streets on many occasions since her first acquaintance with the city in 1968. . A trip to the Con Foster Museum in Traverse City provided valuable insights regarding turn-of-the-century Grand Traverse Bay and its resorts.

Donna has lived all of her life in states bordering on the Great Lakes. Her familiarity and fascination with these remarkable inland waters and her residence in the heart of Great Lakes Country provide the perfect background for writing *Great Lakes Romances*®.

MORE GREAT LAKES ROMANCES®

Visit
www.GreatLakesRomances.com
for excerpts and pricing.

Mackinac, *First in the series of Great Lakes Romances*® (Set at Grand Hotel, Mackinac Island, 1895.) Victoria Whitmore is no shy, retiring miss. When her father runs into money trouble, she heads to Mackinac Island to collect payment due from Grand Hotel for the furniture he's made. But dealing with Rand Bartlett, the hotel's manager, poses an unexpected challenge. Can Victoria succeed in finances without losing her heart?

The Captain and the Widow, Second in the series of Great Lakes Romances® (Set in South Haven, Michigan, 1897.) Lily Atwood Haynes is beautiful, intelligent, and alone at the helm of a shipping company at the tender age of twenty. Then Captain Hoyt Curtiss offers to help her navigate the choppy

246

waters of widowhood. Together, can they keep a new shipping line—and romance—afloat?

Sweethearts of Sleeping Bear Bay, Third in the series of Great Lakes Romances® (Set in the Sleeping Bear Dune region of northern Michigan, 1898.) Mary Ellen Jenkins has successfully mastered the ever-changing shoals and swift currents of the Mississippi, but Lake Michigan poses a new set of challenges. Can she round the ever-dangerous Sleeping Bear Point in safety, or will the steamer—and her heart—run aground under the influence of Thad Grant?

Charlotte of South Manitou Island, Fourth in the series of Great Lakes Romances ® (Set on South Manitou Island, Michigan, 1891-1898) Charlotte Richards, fatherless at age eleven, thought she'd never smile again. But Seth Trevelyn, son of South Manitou Island's lightkeeper, makes it his mission to show her that life goes on, and so does true friendship. Together, they explore the World's Columbian Exposition in far-away Chicago where he saves her from a near-fatal fire. When he leaves the island to create a life of his own in Detroit, he realizes Charlotte is his one true love. Will his feelings be returned when she grows to womanhood?

Aurora of North Manitou Island, Fifth in the series of Great Lakes Romances® (Set on North Manitou Island, Michigan, 1898-1899.) With her new husband, Harrison, lying helpless after an accident on stormy Lake Michigan, Aurora finds marriage far from the glorious romantic adventure she had anticipated. And when Serilda Anders appears out of his past to tend the light and nurse him to health, Aurora is certain her marriage is doomed. Maybe Cad Blackburn, with the ready wit and silver tongue, is the answer. But it isn't right to accept the safe harbor he's offering. Where is the light that will guide her through troubled waters?

Bridget of Cat's Head Point, Sixth in the series of Great Lakes Romances® (Set in Traverse City and the Leelanau Peninsula of Michigan, 1899-1900.) When Bridget Richards leaves South Manitou Island to take up residence on Michigan's mainland, she suffers no lack of ardent suitors. Nat Trevelyn wants desperately to make her his bride and the mother of his two-year-old son. Attorney Kenton McCune showers her with gifts and rapt attention. And Erik Olson shows her the incomparable beauty and romance of a Leelanau summer. Who will finally win her heart?

Queen City Candy Shoppe (excerpted from Rosalie of Grand Traverse Bay), Seventh in the series of Great Lakes Romances® (Set in Traverse City, Michigan, 1900.) Soon after Rosalie Foxe arrives in Traverse City for the summer of 1900, she stands at the center of controversy. Her aunt and uncle are about to lose their confectionery shop, and Rosalie is being blamed. Can Kenton McCune, a handsome, Harvard-trained lawyer, prove her innocence and win her heart?

Isabelle's Inning, Encore Edition #1 in the series of Great Lakes Romances® (Set in the heart of Great Lakes Country, 1903.) Born and raised in the heart of the Great Lakes, Isabelle Dorlon pays little attention to the baseball players patronizing her mother's rooming house—until Jack Weatherby moves in. He's determined to earn a position with the Erskine College Purple Stockings, and a place in her heart as well, but will his affections fade once he learns the truth about her humiliating flaw?

Jenny of L'Anse Bay, Special Edition in the series of Great Lakes Romances® (Set in the Keweenaw Peninsula of Upper Michigan in 1867.) Eager to escape the fiery disaster that leaves her home in ashes, Jennifer Crawford sets out on an adventure to an Ojibway Mission on L'Anse Bay. In the wilderness, her affections grow for a native people very different from herself—especially for the chief's son, Hawk. Together, can they overcome the differences of their diverse cultures, and the harsh, deadly weather of the North Country?

Elizabeth of Saginaw Bay, Pioneer Edition in the series of Great Lakes Romances® (Set in the Saginaw Valley of Michigan, 1837.) The taste of wedding cake is still sweet in Elizabeth Morgan's mouth when she sets out with her bridegroom, Jacob, from York State for the new State of Michigan. But she isn't prepared for the untamed forest, crude lodgings, and dangerous diseases that await her there. Desperately, she seeks her way out of the forest that holds her captive, but God seems to have another plan for her future.

Unlikely Duet—Caledonia Chronicles—Part 1 in the series of Great Lakes Romances® (Set in Caledonia, Michigan, 1905.) Caroline Chappell practiced long and hard for her recital on the piano and organ in Caledonia's Methodist Episcopal Church. She even took up the trumpet and composed a duet to perform with Joshua Bolden, an ace trumpet player whom she'd long admired. Now, two days before the performance, it looks as if her recital plans, and her relationship with Joshua are hitting sour notes. Will she be able to restore harmony in time to save her musical reputation?

Butterfly Come Home—Caledonia Chronicles—Part 2 in the series of Great Lakes Romances® (Set in Caledonia and Calumet, Michigan, 1905-06.) Deborah Dapprich's flighty ways had earned her the nickname, "Butterfly," in childhood. Now, as a young woman of eighteen in the year 1905, her impetuous wanderings brought unanticipated trouble. A marriage of convenience to her childhood friend seemed the only way out. Tommy Rockwell knew that life with his Butterfly would never be dull, but he wasn't prepared for the challenges of his new bride. From Caledonia to Calumet he pursued her, only to discover that he was running second to her first love, the theater. Would she ever light long enough for his love, and the will of God, to work their way into her heart?

Fayette—A Time to Love, Eighth in the series of Great Lakes Romances® (Set in Fayette, Michigan, 1868.) The new iron-smelting town of Fayette, Michigan held no promise for sixteen-year-old Lavinia McAdams. The moment she arrived, she took an instant disliking to its muddy streets, acrid smoke, and dirty furnace men. The sooner she could return to her hometown in Canada, the better. Then Huck Harrigan came along to challenge her thinking and soften her iron will. Could she really find happiness in this raw, new town with a "pig iron" Irishman from across the bay?

Fayette—A Time to Laugh, Ninth in the series of Great Lakes Romances® (Set in Fayette, Michigan in 1879.) The greatest love of Flora McAdams' life had always been her love of animals. From girlhood she had made it her mission to care for orphaned wild creatures and hurting family pets in the pig iron town of Fayette. Now, at age eighteen, she has no lack of four-footed patients needing her skill, and no time or thought of romance, until a quiet Norwegian machinist comes to town. Sven Jorgensen hoped his first encounter with the feisty Flora McAdams would be his last. Whether at the village vegetable garden or the town racetrack, he can't seem to avoid her. But time works miracles. And after witnessing her transformation of hurting, homeless canines into healthy, loving pets, his own heart is transformed as well. Can he somehow convince her that he has much more than friendship in mind for their future?

Fayette – A Time to Leave, Tenth in the series of Great Lakes Romances® (Set in Fayette, Michigan, 1885-1891.) At age fourteen, Violet Harrigan encounters dual tragedies: the death of her father, and the resulting need to move several miles north to Fayette. The situation is more than she can bear. But a true friend sticks closer than a brother. Guy Legard visits Violet faithfully. Months turn into years, and the seed of friendship blossoms into love. Then Guy disappears into the woods for several long months and Violet turns her attention to a suave and debonair newcomer, Reggie Vanderveen. Will he steal her away to a new life of excitement in Boston, or can Guy rekindle the flame of enduring love?

Bluebird of Brockport, A Novel of the Erie Canal (Set in western New York State and on the Erie Canal, 1830) Dreams of floating on the Erie Canal have flowed through Lucina Willcox's mind since childhood. Yet once her family has purchased their boat and begins their journey, they meet with one challenge after another. An encounter with a towpath rattlesnake threatens her brother's life. A thief attempts to break in and steal precious cargo. Heavy rain causes a breach and drains the canal of water. Lucina comforts herself with thoughts of Ezra Lockwood, her handsome childhood friend, and discovers a longing to be with him that she just can't ignore. Can she have a future with Ezra and still hold onto her canalling dream? Ezra Lockwood's one goal in life is to build and captain his own canal boat, but two years into the construction of his freight hauler, funds run short. With his goal temporarily stalled, and Lucina Willcox back in his life, his priorities begin to change. Can he have both his dreams — his own boat, and Lucina as his bride?

For the Love of Roses (Set in western New York State, 1984) Reeling from the loss of her parents in a tragic auto accident, Carey McIlwain resigns her teaching job to take up the reigns of the family florist business, unaware of the challenges that await her. Gavin Jack, the darkly handsome rose supplier threatens to cut off deliveries due to lack of payment. Alex Hensley, the college botanist, wants more than friendship from their casual dates. Her younger brother Todd, who is supposed to step into the business after graduating with his Master's degree, develops a disabling addiction that threatens both his and Carey's future. Can she somehow weather the storms to find security, satisfaction, and that special someone who will steal her heart?

MORE DONNA WINTERS TITLES

Picturing Fayette Fayette Historic Townsite in the Upper Peninsula of Michigan offers visitors a step back in time to a nineteenth century company town. Here, nestled beneath a towering limestone bluff on Lake Michigan, the Jackson Iron Company operated two iron smelting furnaces. From December 25, 1867 to December 1, 1890, hot iron poured forth into casting houses, was cooled and separated into "pigs," and shipped to Ohio aboard schooners. Today, several original structures give testimony to Michigan's industrial past—from the laborers' log cabin, to the managers' salt box homes, to the "Big White House" on the bluff that was occupied by the superintendent. In the center of all these stands the working core of the once-thriving village—the furnace stacks, casting houses, company store, warehouse, town hall, company office, machine shop, and hotel. Through the pages of this book, tour this fascinating open air museum that offers million-dollar views of the harbor, bay, and quaint remnants from nearly 150 years ago. Quotes from newspapers of that era serve as captions, bringing the town to life. Fayette Historic Townsite is without a doubt one of the best-preserved company towns in America and a gem of Michigan history that is unlike any other.

Adventures with Vinnie Handsome. Affectionate. In need of a forever home. And we were in need of another rescue dog. Thus began our Adventures with Vinnie.

From his first day to his last, the only predictable thing about Vinnie was his unpredictability. Loving and loyal, an escape artist to rival Houdini, and a genuinely comical fellow, his antics will make you laugh, give you a fright (but only for a moment), and melt your heart.

So join us, won't you? With Vinnie, there's never a dull moment!

~~~

Having retired to the Upper Peninsula of Michigan, Fred and Donna Winters decided to choose older shelter dogs for their family pets—dogs not easily placed because of their age. When an opportunity arose in March of 2012 to add a Lab/Dobie mix to their family, they didn't hesitate. Nearly forty years of dog parenting had given them confidence that they could provide a safe, loving home for this senior pet fallen on hard times.

They hadn't anticipated the likes of Vinnie.

Learn how that loving shelter dog with bright, longing eyes, led to adventures never expected the day they welcomed him into their lives!

This book contains twelve full-color photographs of Vinnie and his family.

~~~

A Walk in the Valley—Christian encouragement for your journey through infertility by Julie Arduini, Heidi Glick, Elizabeth Maddrey, Kym McNabney, Paula Mowery, and Donna Winters

Everyone's journey through infertility is different. Even women who have the same physical problems will have different courses of treatment, different responses, and different emotional ups and downs as they walk this path. But we also have so much in common: the hurt, anger, frustration, pain, sorrow, hope and joy that we have experienced along the way. We are women who have experienced infertility. Some of us have gone on to conceive, others have adopted, and others remain childless. All of us have found peace in the loving arms of our Father God at the end of our journey. We want to share our experiences and thoughts with you. It is our hope and prayer that you'll be encouraged. This devotional workbook starts with how each woman discovered her infertility, then explores the diagnostic testing pursued, how they processed the official diagnosis, what decisions had to be explored regarding treatment, their experiences during infertility treatment (including pregnancy, miscarriage, and childbirth), and finishes with their experiences in remaining childless, adoption, foster care, child sponsorship, and the emotional healing regardless of the outcome of their infertility journey. Each devotional has a Scripture focus and questions for thought and discussion. 228 pages

Find all of Donna Winters' titles at:

www.GreatLakesRomances.com